THE DIVINE COMEDY II BY BEATRICE

by Ingrid Heller

**There
are dead and living among us.
Some know it, some do not. Some living live ordinary lives,
completing with their responsibilities, given by society's standards.
Others complete with their duties but are seeking more to life. They
know there is something missing. The living who dare to live and
follow the unknown patterns of their destiny, and beyond, are few.
Ingrid Heller is one of the few. It takes the "Hell of a Woman" to
follow the heart and yet, to complete with responsibilities. The
true story of Love and Hope, Faith and Action.
It all started in the polluted downtown of
Santiago de Chile in the late eighties
of the twentieth
century.**

ISBN 1-4033-3715-2

This book is printed on acid free paper.

1stBooks – rev. 7/25/01

CONTENTS

PART FOUR: OPUS FEMINUM

THIS BOOK IS DEDICATED TO MY CHILDREN, FRIENDS, RELATIVES, AND TO EVERYONE I AM TO MEET. IT IS, ESPECIALLY, DEDICATED TO YOU!

PART ONE

CREATION

Ingrid Heller

The First Six Days

Written by Dagmar Meier

The humid wind brushes Ingrid's honey blond hair, to reveal her high forehead, soft and almost free of wrinkles transparent white skin. She selects each step carefully, attempting to avoid puddles on the clayish country road. In the middle of Chilean winter, moist, unpredictable, as it was six years ago when she moved to this location for good. She walks toward a piece of land she worked, toward a house she built, toward a place she left two years later. She felt at this moment like a defeated warrior, or a dreamer, not knowing what the next moment brings, just as it felt those few years ago. Nobody could understand why she has chosen this country to settle in, why she has left the comfort of Canadian city life, with a beautiful house, garden, places for children to play and go to, a school around the corner, all wonderful securities her life offered. Instead of giving herself some time after a divorce, she jumps into another marriage. Of course, Ingrid had all kinds of reasons that her friends learned to accept eventually, yet, when she was leaving with her new Chilean hubby, three children from her previous marriage, three pet german shepherds and ten suitcases, her friends questioned Ingrid's state of mind.

" Why don't you go to visit first, check it out? Why do you burn all bridges?" , they suggested a number of times.

How could they understand the power of commitment to a change? It is like a new lifetime. It has to be one hundred percent. Even before Ingrid met her husband, she felt a magnetic pull toward South America, toward west coast, somewhere, where the sword shaped country was.

She did it, having no idea what the real cause was, what the future was to bring. She lived every moment of each time, again, and all over again.

The muddy road had less holes as she and her companion Patricia were coming closer to the parcela number six.

Patricia had very little to say. She was a local girl, a daughter of neighbours and friends. By now Ingrid knew everything about her husband and the excitement over a pregnancy and plans for an immediate future. The first three days of Ingrid's visit were spent around this small town and its people.

"Señora Ingrid, did you notice a clear view of Cordillera?"

Ingrid looks at Patricia briefly, with softness in her eyes. Then she stops for a moment, gazing at the surroundings and not too distant Cordillera de Los Andes. Memories are coming back, like an inundating river that damaged so much in the country in the winter of 1982. What a year it was!

3

"I always enjoyed the view here, the air, the sound of crickets, frogs and birds. Patricia, I loved it here, but, to stay here became impossible. I couldn't get out of this mud to give birth to Maria in the hospital on most of the days of my labour. I couldn't go through something like that again! Andrew had to be born in Canada! It was much harder to leave Chile than Canada. We planned on coming back... I had unfinished business here... Just don't ask me what it is, I don't know myself, Patricia."

Both women continue on the road. Patricia stops.

"Can you recognize it, Señora Ingrid?"

Ingrid looks ahead in disbelief.

"What happened to the trees, the orchard we've planted? Patricia, they cut down the trees along the canal! It looks so bare! Why had someone taken them away?"

"Señora, the new owner needed to plant grape vines. He left your old house and lives in your big one. He spoke proudly of a good job you've done on it."

Ingrid hears Patricia's voice from a distance, its volume fading away. She stands by the old willow tree, being caressed by its long thin branches. Staring into nothingness she hears the voices of her children, barking of dogs. Her fingers are disappearing into the soil, planting, weeding, bleeding. Clothes she washed by hand are hanging dry in the sun. The baby Maria is resting in her basket under this tree, being entertained by its swinging branches.....'Someone is stealing your corn!', warns the neighbour....'They're not sincere with you, Señora!', says another. 'Why don't your relatives help you more, Señora?', says everyone.........another chicken died, another puppy.... rats are eating the food supply.... the last batch of flour was used up for bread making, the last portion of yeast..... neighbour sends ox tails for the soup.....' How long will it take, Mommy?'...' Sorry, children, we must give it to the dogs, they haven't eaten for three days.'...' Mom, Baron died this morning!'.... 'What? I gave him a water last night! Where is he?'....' On his way to the dog house, Mom. He made it a half way.'.... First grave by the lily garden....Another night with little sleep. Another UFO. Why are they here? ....So much blood running down my thighs. Oh, God, this child must live!.... They were so kind in the hospital - no charges...

Ingrid embraces the willow tree. "Oh, my faithful friend, you know it all!"

"Are you all right, Señora Ingrid? You're crying and talking to the tree!"

"Patricia, this tree knows the whole story, yet, it cannot speak. It talked to my baby Maria. It witnessed the baptism of my four children. This tree somehow kept on saying to me that I had to be in this country. I wish I knew why."

"Our city women wouldn't put up with what you had put up with. I am sure there is something very special here for you..... Do you want to walk back now?"

Ingrid takes a little moment yet to look back at her former home. It couldn't possibly be the last time, and, she knew it. She may be back to visit with all the children and her husband. She reaches into her heavy jacket's pocket and takes out a camera to take a few pictures. This act took her over a threshold, giving her a distance of time. She was a tourist.

Above: The road toward Ingrid's former home in the Chilean countryside.

Next: Hiking to the area of the gold mines nearby

Three days later: July 12, 1988.

Ingrid and Patricia are sitting on a bed in a downtown Santiago hotel. The persistent cough stops all possible verbal communication for quite a while until a thin white cloud gradually disappears.

Ingrid rushes to the window to open it but Patricia quickly gets up and holds the window closed.

"The smoke is from outside, Señora. Students had been demonstrating against the Junta government again. Police used the gas. This one will probably clean us out well."

"What do you mean, Patricia?"

"We'll be evacuating a lot, but, luckily, we have a bathroom.".

"Patricia, I am little bit confused now. We'll hide inside a bathroom during an evacuation? Evacuation for what?"

"If you'll excuse me, Señora, I must go!" and Patricia runs toward a bathroom door.

Ingrid stands there with a wide smile over her face, having no more language barrier. Familiar noises became a clear answer to her question.

In a short while Patricia steps out stating "It was worth it!"

"I thought the demonstration was against the government, Patricia!"

"The government members should live in this neighborhood. They're full of shit. I owe them something after all. The pregnancy made me so constipated, it took a bomb to relieve it." Patricia keeps on smiling and laughing.

"Don't laugh, Patricia, I am next!" and Ingrid was gone at the place where poor, rich, young, old, and people of all kinds and races go at least a few times a day.

Few times? Not in downtown of Santiago on this historical evening of July 12, 1988!

What had the next day to offer?

Let us not worry about tomorrow. Let us enjoy the moment of now. Ingrid knows the meaning of these words well. She had to learn quickly over the past few years. Otherwise, she might break down.

Right now she enjoys the wide mirror with the reflection of ceramic tiles covering all walls and a floor. Bathrooms, definitely, should always be nicely decorated.

In a meanwhile, Patricia rests on a bed, making a few notes in a note book where all the appointments were schedules for Ingrid's meetings for the following day.

"Isn't the name of this hotel Libertador? Don't you feel liberated, Patricia?" says Ingrid to Patricia into a mirror reflection, having already the bathroom door open. "Do you think that the demonstration will accomplish more than this?"

"Chileans want democracy, Señora."

"Are they ready, prepared?"

"What do you mean, Señora Ingrid?"

"You see, Patricia, with democracy there is a responsibility. It is time consuming to keep up with all information, to elect the right party, the right leader. It is a different kind of freedom: with responsibility. Are Chileans ready?"....

"I never thought about it that way. We are tired of a military regime!"

"They kept the country out of trouble from the outside. They couldn't protect you from the inside power - the Church." The second sentence was said with irony in voice.

"I can't believe you're saying these words, Señora!" Patricia shows an evident upset. "I always thought you were a religious woman!"

"Patricia, my religion is my personal inner journey. Yes, it does manifest on the outside. I pray daily, I have a relationship with our Creator through nature, people. I recognize a value of religious archetypes, I had my children baptized, I got married in church. Indeed, you can say that I am a religious person, but, I do not like to be controlled by any dogma or a belief. Life itself is sacred. I honour human being, nature, goodness. Patricia, Catholic Church is a political party, in my opinion. And, it has got its foothold in South America!"

"The Cardinal is coming...."

"When?" Ingrid looks worried.

"Sometime this week. There will be an important meeting in Concepción."

"Let us hope and pray then for a good outcome. It is a crucial time, Patricia."

"Señora, is there something that you know and none of us know? I mean, in Canada you must hear all kinds of news!"

"I gave up on media a long time ago. When we stay away from any kind of programming, another source of information will be available. I dare to call it truth. First, we have to be truthful to ourselves. Before believing anything, we must consult our intuition. We have to be cautious at all times. Ego steps between our thoughts. It teaches us as it misguides and confuses us. It becomes our enemy and a friend at the same time. Do you remember Jesus' saying 'Love your enemies?' We learn from our enemies much more than from our friends. We grow faster among opposition. Individuals, and countries alike, should go through this process."

Patricia is silent for a while, thinking about Ingrid's words.

"Señora, is any country ready for democracy? I mean, you live in a democratic country, you must know!"

Ingrid smiles gently.

"Do I know? In these times probably none."

Then she sits right across from Patricia, takes both her hands, looks lovingly into her eyes and then onto her little belly that is showing some imaginary signs of early pregnancy.

"When your child will reach teens, it will be a part of a country that a whole world will watch in awe. If any country has a special destiny, it is Chile."

"How can you speak this prophetically? In what sense?"

"I feel it will have some special leadership. Democratic and theocratic at the same time."

"Señora, now you got me confused.....what do you mean?"

"Consciousness, Patricia, is the key to the change. In the future we'll have enlightened leaders and citizens. Wouldn't that be ideal?"

"The world is corrupt now, isn't it?"

"You got that right! But we can change it. You, me, them, every newborn can change it one day!"

"But how do you go about it?"

"You cannot change others, but you can change yourself, your attitude. Work on yourself! Become! You are looking at forty-two year old woman, still learning to become. It is a big task for all of us, Patricia."

Then Ingrid turns to uncover her bed, reaching for the nightgown under the pillow.

"Do you want to use the bathroom first, Patricia?"

"I am already using it, Señora!" says Patricia's voice from the room full of ceramic tiles.

"It looks like this is gonna be a hell of a night!", answers Ingrid.

A few more turns, a few more runs. Who can sleep during this busy night? Once in a while a conversation carried on.

"Are you happy in your marriage, Señora Ingrid?", asks Patricia's tired voice.

"Yes, I am. How about you?"

"My husband is the first man I've ever had. I like being married. .How did it feel for you when you got married the third time?"

"This wedding ceremony was special.The pastor who married us knew me. At first, he didn't want to wed us. He kept on saying that this man wasn't for me. Then Verne assured him that he wants to help me to raise my children, to be my partner for life and that he would support me in my endeavors. Pastor friend consented then."

"Your husband is very handsome. Is he good with your children?"

"Very good, Patricia. He also sent me on this trip... .on our honeymoon in Europe he gave me this trip when we were visiting Domo in Florence. I will never forget that moment and the feelings associated with it. We kept on looking at the painting of Dante Alighieri by Domenico di Michelino with images of Hell, Purgatory and Paradise, few Florentian buildings and a tall strong featured Dante in the front with the crown of laurels on his head, wearing a red robe and holding a book - The Divine Comedy. We were somehow fascinated by Dante's face. He radiated wisdom, knowledge, commitment, love, devotion, sadness. He was a man of exile, trying to enlighten people. A great poet!"

"Tell me more about him!"

"I don't know much. His writings were inspired by love for Beatrice whom he saw while very young and never forgot her. When he saw her next time, he was already married, or she wasn't available. Something like that. He was an educator, writer, was involved in cultural, financial and political movement of Florence and when his party lost, he had to go into exile, wandering place to place, until he ended up in Ravenna, where he continued writing. Love for Beatrice was of pure and divine nature and she, as his complimentary female, kept on guiding him throughout the writing of The Divine Comedy. This happened in the late twelve hundreds."

"Do you think that the painting inspired your husband to send you here?"

"I wondered about that, Patricia. He kept on repeating it since then, until I booked a flight. He actually said that he would like me to go to Chile as soon as possible."

"Did he give you any reason?"

"He said that I had some business to finish here, some unresolved situations and that it would be nice for me to get in touch with my friends from whom I wasn't getting any communication for some time. He knew I worried."

"Did you, Señora?"

"Naturally, Patricia! I wrote letters, sent them registered and, no word. Yes, I was concerned."

"Strange, isn't it? We've written too and never got any answer. At times we thought you moved or that something had happened."

"Some things are unexplainable, Patricia. Well, aren't you getting sleepy?"

No answer. Patricia was asleep. Ingrid watches her for a while, thinking of the days when she was making surprise visits to give her a hand with some housework. There was always so much to do. Patricia's help was treasured. Friendship grew despite the age difference. Now, she rests peacefully in a warm room, showered by the warm water, comfortable. A faithful companion.

Ingrid on her honeymoon in Florence in April 1988.

Calle Ahumada with Agustinas on July 13, 1988, with demonstrators in the background.

The Seventh Day

Santiago, July 13, 1988

Ingrid got up early in the morning, trying to be as quiet as possible, not to awaken Patricia, who's been up so many times during the night. She checked the agenda book with one appointment in the morning right in downtown and other two for the afternoon in the industrial area of Santiago. She decided to get ready in the meanwhile, before Patricia gets up.

One glance into the mirror to see how much puffiness there is left in her eyelids and under the eyes, what the darkness of the night has done to the whiteness of Ingrid's body. She keeps on looking at her image, questioning the reality of what she was seeing. There was no sign of a sleepless night! She looked to herself more beautiful than ever. What is going on?, she wondered.

Patricia was sitting up in her bed.

"Señora, you are looking so beautiful today!"

"Beautiful?"

"Yes, Señora! Radiant!"

"Let me see!", and Ingrid steps back into the bathroom, closing the door behind. She looks into the mirror again. Yes, her image is radiant. And there is a very vital feeling all over her body. She glides her gown off her shoulders, slides it lower and lower, uncovering the fullness of her breast, which looked like this only during the first months of pregnancies. The last time Ingrid examined herself in this way was before the honeymoon, when she tried her new nightie, and long before that during her early teens. She had to acknowledge her exceptional beauty. The gown falls on the tile floor, just to form a silky carpet so she can walk further from the mirror, to observe more of unveiled feminine beauty. She lifts up her arms over her head, flexes them behind her long neck. The Goddess is back! From every angle the sight was more than pleasing. Ingrid takes a deep breath - in regret. Her husband is not here to enjoy and feast on that multidimensional slender fullness, to give her the pleasure of sharing the harvest of her fruit. She thirsts for a touch, a physical contact. A substitute of a shower was a sad replacement she had to settle for, but, after all,   thousands of tiny fingers energizing and covering epidermis garment of that body satisfied a longing for intimacy.

The phone rings. Patricia picks it up. It was uncle Manuel. He apologized for not being able to take Ingrid to her appointments. Due to vehicular restriction to control pollution, he could not show up on the road with his licence plate number. This changed the day's programme. Patricia was very efficient in managing Ingrid's affairs and booked the afternoon commitments for the following day.

"This gives us some extra time in downtown, Patricia. We can do some smart shopping. Let me call home. I miss my husband!"

"Your husband should see you today, Señora. You always looked feminine and attractive, but today you look incredibly special."

Ingrid smiles softly. "Thank you for your compliments, Patricia. I wish they came from my bride-groom's mouth!"

"Call him!"

Ingrid was lucky to get through the lines.

"Verne, how are you? I wish you were here, I miss you so much!........Verne? Are you there?"

"Yee, I am listening.", was the answer.

"How is everything, are the children alright?"

"Everything is fine. We'll meet you at the airport next week. The same time of arrival?"

"Yes, darling. I love you! I miss you!"

No answer.

"Verne? Do you hear me?"

"Yes, I do. I cannot say too much here. People are listening."

"You cannot say to your wife that you loved her? I don't believe this, Verne! You said it at the altar and everyone could hear it, including them!"

There was no comment.

"Give my love to the children! I have to get some gifts for them yet. You still want the Argentinian leather jacket, right?"

"Only if it is possible."

"Of course, it is. I am leaving for Mendoza in two days."

"Is it safe to go there, Ingrid? I hope I don't have to worry about you!"

"Absolutely safe! Patricia's cousin Alberto is coming with me and we are taking a bus together with his father, who is visiting his niece there. People are kind here."

"Enjoy the trip!", says Verne.

"Next time we'll travel together. Bye, love!"

Ingrid hangs up and stares for a while out the window, not paying any attention to the walls of dark gray color, neither the asbestos roof of the lower neighbouring building. Even the sky was colourless.

"You look sad, Señora.", says concerned Patricia.

"Sometimes, I don't understand my husband. His moods swing one day to the other. I am disappointed! He was cold!"

"Men don't show their emotions easily, Señora."

"Remember, Patricia, when I told you about my fears prior to this trip?"

"I remember well. You were afraid that something might happen to you. You thought you would die!"

"Right! Verne actually tried to talk me out of the trip a day before the flight: honey, if you feel that you might die, I don't want you to go. It is better to lose fifteen hundred dollars than you. Stay home and forget about the trip."

"Yes, Señora Ingrid, and you chose to find out what the fear was all about and went anyway."

"Right! So, here I am. Don't you think my husband should be a little bit concerned?"

"I think he trusts you, Señora, and must know that you're brave and clever."

"I'm probably worrying about nothing. You're right, Patricia. He is trusting me, otherwise he wouldn't send me here. Before the wedding he was terribly insecure and always jealous, and all that without a reason. He does want me to enjoy this trip. I am going to do just that! Ready for breakfast?"

"Starving! There is nothing left in me, all is gone!"

A click of the door knob cut into the middle of light giggles, that resonated in the large hallway. Both women were descending on foot to the lower floor dining room.

A waiter shows Ingrid to their table and as soon as she and Patricia sit down, offers them coffee.

"Not today. We'll have juice instead.", says Ingrid.

"Señora, all the men are looking at you!"

"Is there something wrong with my hair?"

"They're looking at your radiance!"

"Oh, right, I forgot that I was radiant today. Maybe we should tell them that my husband doesn't give a damn, or that last night we kept on flushing the toilet."

"Cheer up, Señora. What will we do this afternoon?"

"I thought of going to the Canadian Embassy and give them my next contact numbers, in case the children need to reach me."

"Good idea! It is on the same street just two blocks away. It would be my first time on Canadian territory."

"We'll have a nice leisure afternoon, Patricia. The day will be colourful despite the sky's grayness."

It takes very little to make Ingrid feel enthusiastic. When she was a child, she preferred to laugh, play, dance and sing. Sadness brought only suffering and dark thoughts. She refused to dwell on nightmares and disliked scary fairy tales. Why does anyone want to frighten little children?, she thought. Adults seemed so detached when she was growing up. When she finally left her native Bohemia twenty years ago, a new world opened up before her eyes. She fell in love with Canada. Love for a country can be as strong as love for people. Ingrid knew about falling in love and being in love. She was a love.

Downtown of Santiago is a very busy place, especially in the heart of city, where hotel Libertador is located. It is on the street Bernardo O'Higgins, commonly called Alameda, where both universities are located and all the important streets are leading to.

Ingrid and Patricia began their walk toward Calle Ahumada, where the Embassy is located. Ingrid keeps very quiet, minding her own business. She learned a long time ago that an eye contact can provoke a reaction she may not desire. She practiced this very faithfully. Besides, the available space to get ahead was limited. At times, she had to break away from Patricia's arm to avoid a collision with another human being. Ingrid walks faster to reach to her destination.

"Señora, slow down, please! You're going in the wrong direction. The Embassy is over there! " Patricia is pointing into the opposite direction than Ingrid had chosen.

"I know where I am going, Patricia. Just follow me.", answers Ingrid calmly.

Patricia looks at Ingrid with surprise, thinking that perhaps Ingrid wants to go somewhere else first and, keeps on walking with her, arm in arm.

There is a group of young people displaying banners with NO. They are being questioned by police.

Ingrid stops for a while.

"What is going on here, Patricia?"

"The students have a winter vacation. Yesterday's demonstration was the beginning of protests against our government. They say NO to Junta."

"No arrests?"

"Not as much anymore, Señora. Everyone wants peace."

Ingrid continues walking in her chosen direction. She looks ahead and notices a tall man of an upright posture, standing at the entrance of a building near street Huérfanos. Ingrid is drawn to him, feeling a strong magnetic current. ..... Who is he? He is so special!....

Recognizing the force of a bond to this man, she feels a guilt:... No, I cannot look at this man. My husband gave me this trip, I am a married woman. I must not look at this man!....

The first effort was quite successful until she comes closer. Instead of being forty meters away, she was two meters near him.   .

...... Just one more look and then I'll forget him. I must forget him. I cannot possibly look at him. I am a married woman....

One more treat. What a special face! Strong, raugh and gentle, proud and humble..... What is he doing here? He is not from here! He is looking into the distance, waiting for someone. I feel a fascination for this man!....

Ingrid looks away, being aware that Patricia was a silent observer of this mental dialogue. No more looks.

Ingrid is coming closer to Plaza d'Armas.

A crowd of pedestrians had suddenly become thinner. Surprised Ingrid looks at her companion.

"I can't believe this, Patricia. The Embassy is in the other direction of Calle Ahumada. How could I get this disoriented?"

"I told you, Señora, but you wouldn't listen!"

"You told me?"

"Yes! You said you knew where you were going!"

"Strange, I don't know why I did that. Well, let's just go back the same way and we'll be there in no time. We're in no hurry."

Arm in arm, Patricia at Ingrid's right, both women take the same route. Ahumada is a major downtown passage, with no traffic. Only at crossings with other streets some vehicles are rushed through. It is a place where all kinds of people can be seen: upper, middle and lower class and where beggars and pick-pockets usually get very lucky. A group of young religious men are walking briskly right in the middle of the passage, to avoid the greater crowds on sidewalks. They attracted Ingrid's attention.

"Who are these men, Patricia? Are they monks?"

Patricia steps very energetically in front of Ingrid, looking sternly into her eyes, blocking her way.

"They're the priests of the Order of Santa Gemita, Señora Ingrid!"

Patricia's voice sounded very authoritarian. How can she answer with so much certainty?, wondered Ingrid. How can she know this?

There was a strange feeling associated with this moment. Ingrid felt compelled to look to her left. A vague figure of a fair colour being is observing her. A powerful presence and a magnetic pull draws her attention further to the left The same man, whom she was fascinated by, looks hypnotically into her eyes. Being only one meter near him, she stands there breathless, observing a beam of milky white light descending onto his head, transforming him into an image of Jesus Christ. The image she cherished since January 21, 1981, when she was thirty four years old. He was looking at Ingrid, embracing her in the white cloud. She hears a mute, yet mentally audible voice: I KNOW YOU. YOU ARE PART OF ME... Ingrid is locked into his eyes, that radiated the deepest confession of love and devotion. With peripheral vision she could see Patricia staring at him, also, being breathless. She was slightly touched by the cloud, that had a form of an ovum. At Ingrid's left some people were trying to pass between Ingrid and him, but, bounced off the invisible wall - the milky white ovum. They walked around Ingrid, continuing on their way toward street Huérfanos. Ingrid takes a deep breath. The white cloud disappears. Ingrid breathed it in. There before her was the same man she saw while walking up the street. One good look at him from head to toe: high forehead, greenish blue eyes, prominent nose, sensual lips, masculine chin, all forming a well put together face, handsome,

16

attractive. Pyramid angled shoulders, trimmed body, groomed, perfect. He holds a briefcase in his left hand. Left hand! No ring!

.... This is the man I'd love in the purest and the most passionate way. He would inspire me to the highest I'd be able to accomplish. He is the one I would cross valleys and oceans and move mountains for...

One more glance over this tall body dressed in black.

Him and Patricia are looking at each other. He is feeling embarrassed under Ingrid's scanning. It's over. He looks at Ingrid, sapping for the air, ready to say something. Ingrid takes Patricia's arm at this very moment and walks away.

An inner dialogue begins:

.... What am I doing? I cannot walk away like that! I must do something!.....

Ingrid looks back, with a happy smile

.... At a least, that I can do. He is so beautiful! He blushes! Oh, what a pure man! I can see him breathing, I can hear his heart beating! He smiles! This is heaven!....

.Ingrid stopped just for a second.

....He is the one I always loved. What am I going to do? I am a married woman. I cannot talk to him ....

Patricia is observing, saying nothing. She is somehow feeling Ingrid's frustration. Both women continue walking down the street. Ingrid looks back one more time, with an even more precious smile he was not to forget. He calls her by the name PAMELA.

Ingrid stops and hesitates. She feels a pain in her heart.It is growing.... It is his pain and doubled by my pain. I am dying, dying, dying.....

One more moment of eye to eye contact, to carry forever in her memory. She walks away. The inner struggle continues until a silent voice says: you'll meet him again when you're both ready. Go back to your life, complete your life with your family. Keep on walking! You're strong, you can do it!

Ingrid did it. She looks only ahead, passing by the demonstrators, looking up to spot a Canadian flag.

"There it is, Patricia! It is on the upper floor. I remember now! I was pregnant with Andrew when I was here last time."

"That was four years ago, wasn't it, Señora?"

"Yes, Patricia. We left Chile at that time. It seems like a long time ago. Time flies so quickly."

Two hours later Patricia and Ingrid are sitting in a dining room. A waiter is bringing two glasses of red wine Ingrid ordered.

Ingrid picks up one glass giving a gesture for the toast.

"To this very unique day" and sips some of it, leaving the glass very full.

Few moments of silence pass.

"How could you walk away from that man, Señora?"

17

"I had to. Please, don't make me regret it. I suffer enough for it."

"You could have at least talked to him, you always talk to people!"

"Duty, Patricia, is a powerful scruple. I have a family. I am a newlywed. I got married only three months ago and my husband trusts me, remember?"

"This man was special! He looked at you in such a powerful way. You must had fallen in love with him!"

Ingrid is observing a reflection of light in the red wine. She lifts up the cup and sips some more. Her brown eyes show more depth than before. Patricia notices that Ingrid is hurting.

"You haven't answered me, Señora Ingrid!", Patricia reminds her.

"It will be hard to return to my husband the way I've been with him, but I'll try. I must try. Life has to be lived moment to moment, we have to do our best in every instant of it. I did my best, for harmony and peace. I did the right thing for the time being, Patricia."

"Who do you think he is?"

"In the rapture we've experienced together I perceived many things about him. I will call him Priest. He should wear a crown. He's got many virtues. A very caring and involved man. He had manuscripts in his briefcase."

"How do you know that, Señora?"

"I felt it. He writes and teaches and speaks several languages. His communication to me was in English."

Patricia opens her eyes very widely, in dismay. "He said something to you?"

"It was telepathic. He also called me Pamela."

"This is strange, Señora....That man loves you! I could feel it. You are his bride!"

Ingrid breaks into tears, trying to cover for it. She is sobbing inside, not being able to keep her torso calm.

"I died this afternoon. I was dying on that street. He was dying with me...."..

"I don't understand, Señora! What do you mean?", asks confused Patricia.

"It was the end, and the beginning. It felt like death, and the rebirth. Everything had changed in that moment."

"In what way?"

"A perception of the world has changed."

Another communion with the wine. Ingrid left the glass pink with a tiny sip.

"What will you do, Señora?"

"Go back to my life, of course. I have a tremendous motivation now. Love for this man will make me stronger."

"Is it possible to love two men?"

"There are different degrees of love. Yes, it is possible."

There is a sadness in Ingrid's eyes.

"You may never meet this man again, Señora. Why didn't he follow you?"

"He is a respecter of free will. He respected my choice. Besides, he was waiting for someone. He couldn't leave the location. That person was about twenty minutes late. It was 15:20 hours. He was waiting for a Chilean, obviously. They're mostly late."

Patricia laughed, acknowledging the truth in Ingrid's comment. She knew her own people well.

Ingrid challenges her companion with another toast of wine.

"A toast to a new beginning, Patricia! A toast to your baby, your hope!"

Both women click the glasses, look into each other's eyes and slowly progress in emptying their cups.

The waiter comes quickly in response to Ingrid's call.

"One more glass for me, please, and for the young lady a glass of fresh water."

In a short while Ingrid raises a glass with red wine, Patricia raises her glass of water. "To our future and to my quest!"

"Will you look for him, Señora Ingrid?"

"This cup is his cup. No matter what it takes, Patricia, I am going to find out who he is and why I met him today. This is a great challenge. Do you realize how many people are there in this world? He is one of billions and I am going to find him!"

Ingrid Heller

PART TWO

The Letter to the Reader

Ingrid Heller

Welcome to My World! My name is Ingrid Heller. I was born in Bohemia in the middle of September 1946. I was obviously conceived after the war, by a couple who were in love with each other. I was their second child. My home town is called Liberec, which means 'libera', or 'freedom'. Our apartment was located on Frýdlant Street, meaning 'free land street'. (about forty years later it was renamed Falcon Street.)

This city of seventy thousand people provided me with a special environment. We basically lived in downtown, yet, enjoyed a large garden with an orchard and a pile of sand, to build our castles and kingdoms, with trees to climb, tall grass to hide in, and a swing that was my favourite.

My two year older brother was a complimentary companion. We played house, competed in drawings and later on we played music together. Eventually, we grew apart. He became an architect but lived only to 39 years of age. Our father passed away when we were very young. Our mother never remarried.

I was a sociable, extroverted and a happy child. At school I got occasionally into trouble for my outspoken nature. I was not made for a controlling communist system. Frequently, I went to the surrounding mountains for the peace and quiet, and communion with nature. There I felt truly free. Playing piano and singing became my daily medicine. Overall, I was one of the best students at school, excelling in everything but history. We were told that some pages in our history books were not the truth anymore. I stopped trusting history. The past didn't really matter.

The city had all kinds of colleges and two faculties. Despite my desire to study the art of glass and crystal making, I was placed to business college. Instead of studying, I dated. The outdoors was much healthier anyway. I enjoyed the study of foreign languages which led into meeting people and to lifetime friendships. After I graduated and worked as a well trained accountant, I auditioned for a local, yet internationally reknown choir, and for the opera chorus. I passed. It enriched my life tremendously.

On August 21, 1968, a tragedy happened. Warsaw pact armies invaded my country. The "Free land" street was terribly violated by tanks and army camions. I was faced with a decision. I chose to leave. My 'pen pals' from western countries offered help. I was on my way to freedom and chose Canada to be my next homeland.

The story you are about to read is a true story. It happened to me. Since the Santiago encounter my life became magic. All I experienced in the vital relationships outside myself, had a deep meaning. I began to read, and live, my own story, my own script. There were messages everywhere. Some of my friends were involved from the beginning of my quest and I, and you, owe them thanks for encouraging me to share it with others. You must understand that I am literally stripping my soul to take you with me on my Journey. I will attempt to select the most important events and leave some untouched, otherwise, the book would be too long. Bare with me and take to yourself that which may relate to you. We all are unique individuals and it takes love and courage to surrender to our soul's guidance and dare to live our own drama, our comedy.

THE DIVINE COMEDY II
BY BEATRICE
written by Ingrid Heller

Popes

I was left alone in Santiago for one day. Patricia had to return to her husband and was to instruct her cousin Alberto where to locate me. I went one more time to the location where I met my Priest, exactly at 15:20, in hope that he might do the same. I knew that he desired to see me again. I could feel his frustration.

During the day I wondered how I'll manage to go on in life with his and my feelings. The connection was established regardless of the distance. His face was continuously reminding itself on the screen of my third eye. This eventually had to stop! Positively, my feet were set on the path and, I needed all clarity I could get. Never had I intended to become another Don Quijote. There was no choice, though. I also had to become my own teacher and had to be sceptic as much as possible to remain grounded.

In the evening of doing nothing after the first seven days of creation of my own unresolved puzzle, I had rested. God rested on the seventh day. I was beyond that. Curiosity about the outside world made me to push the button. Television became a source of information on that day. The cardinal was already in Chile. I guess, the priests we saw were coming to the Liberation Theology convention. I could hear the trumpets of Revelation: the change was on the way. What ever was to happen! We all strive in changes with great challenges. I was ready with my modest breast plate.

Alberto arrived on the following morning. I met him at the bus terminal and within hours we were on the bus to Mendoza. I gave Alberto the window seat. His father Manuel sat behind me. We talked little on the way. Los Andes have very little of the beauty of the Canadian Rockies. Aconcagua seemed unsignificant and so was the famous ski resort Portillo. Argentinian territory had a couple of interesting highlights, such as a natural formation in the rock looking like a tiger. And there was Mendoza, the city of tango, exiles, leather and dealers. Everybody knew somebody who had the best prices of leather jackets. After checking two hotels we had to pick four star. It was comfortable. Alberto had a bed by the window, I had mine by the door. We both shared equal distance to the bathroom, that needed extra scraping. The door knob was broken. We simply had to trust each other. Considering that Alberto came along to make sure that I am safe, I trusted.

Tired and hungry, we rushed to look for a fast food place. We found a small restaurant around the corner. Before we took the first bite, two men offered us the best deals in leather. One of them was going to take us there on his motorcycle. This was Friday night.

We wanted to go dancing to Tangomania with Manuel the next day. We could hardly wait. If you ever danced tango, you may as well fantasize dancing it in Argentina. Well, I did.

The television had only two stations with very boring programs. We gave up on it easily and slept well through the night.

Quick shower, quick grooming and we were on our way to the main floor dining room for breakfast. The moment we locked the door, a group of seven young priests are turning a corner, being led by a cardinal who was blind. He almost touched me with his white cane. He was about forty, the priests averaged thirty-two. For a while I was compelled to say something to the cardinal, but the words had left my tongue and I stood there in silence. All his companions were handsome. Doubtlessly, they looked Spanish. They began to enter a room next to us, one by one. It had to be a room reserved for Snow White and the seven dwarves. Or, did they actually share beds? One of them was a real man. He couldn't get his eyes off me. He was cute!

Alberto made his comment in the elevator.

"We certainly can be at peace with these neighbours!"

"Alberto, I felt an urge."

"I could see that!"

The young man was far too quick with his answers.

"I haven't finished, Alberto!"

I continued the sentence on the way to the dining room. "I had an urge to speak with the blind man."

"The blind man cannot appreciate you, Señora Ingrid."

"Alberto, I had a message for the cardinal. Let's hope that this trip doesn't represent missed opportunities."

"You've made that mistake once already in Santiago on Wednesday, right?"

"How do you know about it?"

"The first thing Patricia said to everyone was about this handsome man whom you fell in love with. Was it really that special?"

"Special is not the correct word. It was divine...."

"Divine? Like Heaven, Paradise?"

"Paradise, Alberto, Paradise."

I reviewed the encounter again. How many more times will I do it?

Luckily the waiter came to take our order. I didn't feel hungry anymore. I ordered a continental breakfast. Alberto ordered eggs and ham.

"Let us plan the day, Alberto. First, we shall find out where the best Tangomania place is and then we'll get a jacket for my husband. After lunch we're free. What do you want to do?"

"With you, anything Señora!"

"We can talk, how about that?"

"Yes, we can start with a talk, Señora Ingrid."

I had never seen Alberto chewing his food so slowly, feeling every piece of flesh with his tongue, turning it, churning it, drinking it.

"Did your mother teach you about digestion and assimilation?"

"Not my mother, but my teachers did."

"Who were your teachers, Alberto?"

"Women, Señora, women."

Alberto continues chewing in the same manner. He loads the next fork with eggs, bringing it closer to his mouth, opening his nostrils to smell it and then slowly taking it in with his full lips, piece by piece. ...A sensual lad! He does it so well. No wonder he looks so healthy and girls like him. He is an attractive man. Only twenty-two! He could be my son. He looks more western European than of Chilean roots.... Finally, he is done.

A similar scene was repeated at lunch. It was a late lunch that stretched into an early supper. It was time to get ready for the night of dancing the tango.

Manuel was to meet us in the lobby at seven. We both were ready, waiting. We heard a car stopping by the entrance. It was a station wagon with the cardinal and priests, all eight of them. How could they fit into the vehicle? Alberto looks at me, with a mischievous smile. Nobody was supposed to read our thoughts!

I was pacing in the lobby back and forth, waiting for Manuel. The cute priest stops and gives me an evaluating look. All the others walked ahead .

"Don't look at me like that, Father!" I said to him, while he was undressing me in his imagination.

"I am not looking at you like that!" he answers.

"Yes, you are!"

"I am not!"

"Father, I am a mother of five children!"

He glances briefly at Alberto.

"I see.... how lovely. Congratulations!"

His companions were waiting for him by the elevator and he proceeded to join them. Then they ascended....

Alberto comes closer to me and whispers over my shoulder: "Now you had your chance to speak, Señora. Did you pass him your message?"

A rascal! A character! He does it again! "I wanted to speak to the blind one!"

"But I told you earlier, Señora,.only a seeing man can appreciate you. This one had eyes to see!"

"Do you have ears to hear, Alberto? I guess you do! Then listen to me! Your comments are funny, but, sometimes I am concerned that you might cause me trouble. Remember, God gave you two eyes, two ears, but only one mouth. Think about it!"

Partially I was to be blamed for this incident. I wore a lovely black dress, black pumps and stockings that I bought in Santiago for tonight's occasion, and I had a red rose satin pin that attracted lots of attention. The young priest was himself.

Manuel arrived. We walked together to the nearest Tangomania. The place looked like a barn, only a part of it was covered by a wooden dance floor. The stage was brightly lit up and a real orchestra played. We danced and danced up to midnight. Then Manuel suggested we should go back to the hotel. The air was charged up. He wanted to avoid trouble. We gladly obeyed.

The moment I walk into our hotel room, I kick off my shoes, feeling a sudden relief.

"Who is going to take a shower first? You or I?", I asked.

No answer. Alberto stands in between a closet door, quiet.

"Alberto, do you want to take a shower now?"

"I need a cold one, Señora..."

I am getting suspicious. Alberto is boxed in the closet. Is he stuck? I walk over to him. He holds a magazine, flipping its pages.

"What are you reading? Did you bring this with you?"

All of a sudden, I notice it was a pornographic magazine. I become upset and reach out agressively for the magazine. "Give this to me! Where did you get this?"

"It was up here in the closet, Señora."

Alberto was telling me the truth. I was thinking about the priests.

"Imagine, Alberto, when priests see this and their superior can't!"

Alberto and I break into laughter. I went over to the dresser and the night table, looking into all of the drawers. They were all empty with the exception of one which had a pen and paper inside.

"What are you looking for, Señora?"

"A Bible! Every Canadian hotel has a Bible. Here they have a pornographic magazine!"

We both laughed even more. Alberto agreed to take a bath first. It was an opportunity for me to look into a confiscated magazine. Even though I was in my third marriage, I knew very little!

Later, when I finished my bath, Alberto was asleep in his bed by the window. I turn off the light and thanked God for a day full of fun. I was looking forward the trip back to Chile in the afternoon. I fell fast asleep.

About one hour later I heard Alberto's whisper: "Señora Ingrid, are you asleep?"
. "Not anymore! What is it, Alberto?" It takes so little to wake me up. It must be mother's syndrome.
"I cannot sleep!" says a bit louder whisper.
"Pray, then!"
"I already did, Señora!"
"Count sheep!" I suggest.
"How do you count sheep?"
"One, two, three, etc., until you run out of sheep!"
"I have never heard of that.
"So count something else. Money, whatever, until you run out of it."
"That would be easy, I already did!"
"Look, Alberto, I want to sleep. Don't bother me anymore, okay?"
It was easy to figure out what was on Alberto's mind. Being young and healthy and inspired. … That damn magazine spoils my sleep!… Under no circumstances was I going to play into Alberto's scheme. I was ignorant, innocent and terribly sleepy.

I was near twighlight zone when I hear a whisper again. "Señora, I still cannot sleep."
I pretend that I hear nothing. I was sound asleep.
Few minutes pass. I became aware of the time. Alberto was tossing and turning in his bed, and yawning aloud.
"Señora, what shall I do?"
"Count your breath! You never run out of that!"
"Do you think that will work?"
"Of course, proven! All meditation groups use it. They fall asleep quickly. Sometimes they snore."
"Do you meditate sometimes, Señora?"
"No time. I am an activist. I do things."
"I like to do things too, Señora!"
I was becoming agitated. This young fellow never quits. Typical man, keeping on trying until he gets what he wants. No matter what, I had to be on top of the situation.
"Do you want me to sing you a lullaby?"
"Only if I can come to your bed." says Alberto quickly.
"Forget it! I don't sleep with men."

"Your husband is a man!"

For a moment I was wondering whether our conversation was amusing, or challenging. Alberto didn't insist on this trip. He was invited to keep me company and take me back to Chile in safety. Did he actually believe that he was to look after my needs? Mine were certainly different from his. Regardless, I had to do something to stay out of trouble.

"All right, Alberto, come to sleep in my bed!"

He throws the covers off and races into my bed. At that very instant I get out of my bed from the other side and run into his bed by the window. We change beds in the same way at least two more times. He might interpret this as foreplay, so I had to change the strategy. I had to be a director and him an actor.

"Alberto, you know you cannot get anywhere this way. You're supposed to be my body guard, not my raper!"

"I am your body guard! I would love to watch over it forever, Señora! You are the woman of my dreams! I secretly loved you!"

"Good try, Alberto! If you don't smarten up, I am going to call a priest for help!"

"That would not help. One was already undressing you in his mind. And they saw the magazine!"

A flash of inspiration! The magazine! Now I am going to use his own weapon against him. What an opportunity to transform darkness into light! The motif of my favourite fairy tales!

Instantly, I became a hell of a woman. Some men used to call me that way. They had no idea about the German meaning of my surname. It was just the opposite of Hell. Duality interplay is behind all evolution and growth and it was available to me right now!

"Alberto...? Would you like to have an unforgettable experience?" I ask in a very nocturnal sedductive voice. I did my best to lower the pitch.

"With you, Señora?" asks excited Alberto.

I am observing his breathing. None of us counted the breath. We couldn't keep up.   "Only under one condition: that you will be a recipient of pleasure, and I will be a giver."

"Oh, Señora! You are such a beautiful and giving woman!"

"The rule is that the recipient cannot touch the giver. You must be submissive."

"This is the dream of my life!"

Quickly, I had to gather all resources from my memory bank and imagination in the domain of lust. I had to think what Alberto would like the most. It had to be like a perfectly wrapped package, with bows and ribbons, with many layers of paper, and if possible, having many scotch tapes, waiting to be opened slowly. Inside had to be a real surprise, such as a gift certificate or a rain cheque.

First I place Alberto in supine position on his bed, making sure he feels comfortable. He tries to vacuum into his nasal passage my personal fragrance. I allowed my hair to caress his face. Then energetically I strip the top sheet of my bed and glide it in front of my body. A special emphasis on sensuality had to be considered at all times. The same sheet I roll into a thick rope, placing it across Alberto's hips, tying it together on the side of the bed. The final knot was completed when Alberto inhaled. I rush into the bathroom for the large towels and tie Alberto's feet together. Remembering Alberto's clothing, I reach for Alblerto's pants in the closet and glide them over my shoulders, shaking my hair over them. Fencing duals had always fascinated me, especially, when the actor was Spanish or French. I draw the belt! I whish it in every direction, looking straight at my subject with all my feline energy. I am tying his hands together. He lets me. He is left to count his breath afterall. I take my winter coat from the closet, lay on my own bed and cover myself. Observing Alberto for a while, I am beginning to feel a genuine compassion for him. He gave me a gift of this most unusual experience I cannot possibly forget, unless, I choose to.

"Good night, Alberto. I hope you know me better now."

"Your husband has a treasure in you. A lucky man!"

Alberto resigned and surrendered. No more whispers. I covered him with my blanket and hoped to sleep at least four hours. The same day we were returning to Santiago by the afternoon bus.

.

It must had been near noon hour when I woke up. I phoned reception. It was eleven. I ordered breakfast through room service. Alberto still sleeps. I had a little hangover from the cigarette smoke in Tangomania place. In a short while there was a knock on the door. I button the coat and, barefoot, open the door. The same young waiter, who served us each time, cheerfully wishes me "Good morning." His facial expression changes quickly, seeing Alberto, who is still tied to his bed. The waiter angrily puts the tray on the dresser, attempting to wake up Alberto with its noise.

"Enjoy your scrambled eggs!" he says and leaves.

Alberto woke up. He said no word about the last night. I untie him and give him his breakfast on the tray.

"Aren't you going to share it with me, Señora?", he says with modesty in his voice.

"I'll wait for our early dinner. The bus leaves at four. I am not hungry yet."

Slowly I began to get our things ready and took plenty of time in the bathroom. Alberto was respectful and not very chatty. Poor lad, he learned his lesson.

We were the only guests in the dining room. The same waiter comes over with his pad and pen and bows to me   "What would Señora like? We can have the chef to prepare a special dish for you."

"I just want lots of vegetables and hardly any meat. Actually, a nice meat broth would be appreciated."

"What ever you desire, Señora!" the waiter says in a very subservient manner.

Then he walks over to Alberto, whom he ignored so well upto then, steps with one foot ahead of the other, looks at him sternly and with superiority in his voice says "And what would the kid like? A glass of milk?"

Alberto was shocked. Him, who was treated yesterday with courtesy, became a second class citizen overnight.

I had to interfere.

"The young man can order for himself. I am sure that chef can prepare something special for him as well."

The waiter bows to me: "Whatever you say, Señora!"

Then he turns to Alberto again and in the same way as before says to him "How about a chicken breast and thighs with sauce to satisfy your taste?"

"An excellent suggestion! Make sure the meat is of a young and fresh chicken. Custard for dessert, please!"

A defeated waiter leaves, with the orders. Alberto looks at me "Are you enjoying yourself, Señora? He thinks I am a chicolo!", waiting for my input.

"You had a good answer for him`", I said with neutrality. We talked a bit. Insignificant comments of simple people. No bitterness, no reminders of the past. When plates were cleared a waiter asks me about a dessert. I told him I'll pass on it, that I had plenty of delicious things to enjoy in the past few days, and asked for the bill. There were no more emotions coming from the waiter. He got a tip he deserved.

We boarded the bus for Santiago. Alberto got his seat by the window, I sat next to him. There were about twenty passengers among whom I noticed a young priest. He carried a very small suitcase and kept to himself. After a couple hours of the bus ride Alberto reached for the chocolate bars we purchased at a kiosk and passed me two of them. I gave one to the priest who was sitting right across the isle. At first he refused with thanks but, when I insisted that he must accept it, he did.

"All good things are much nicer when they're shared, don't you think, Father?" I said to make him feel more comfortable.

"I agree.... Have you enjoyed your stay in Mendoza?"

Alberto looks at me waiting for my answer. I gave him a glance acknowledging his concern, turning to the priest again.

"Yes, it was an interesting visit. Are you from here, Father?"

"No, Señora, I am a Chilean, but I have a parish here."

"Why here, why not in Chile?"

"They need me here."

I noticed a sadness in his voice.

"I can see that. I saw a cardinal with his companions. Have you met them?"

All of a sudden the priest became agitated. "You saw a false Pope!"

"A false Pope? You mean there is a real Pope?"

"Of course there is a real Pope: Juan Pablo Secundo!"

"Who is he, where is he from?" I ask.

"From the Vatican!"

"The blind man?"

"Our Pope is not blind! He can see!" The priest was becoming annoyed.

I had to heal our misunderstanding immediately."Father, I am asking about the man with the white cane. The one I saw!"

"The man is crazy!" says the priest quickly.

"Which man is crazy?"

"The blind one!"

Alberto changed his sitting position, looking directly at both of us, waiting for entertainment. A master word riddler became our grateful audience.

"Why is he crazy, Father?"

"He saw Christ!"

"And that makes him crazy?"

"Nobody can see Christ!"

"Nobody can, Father?" I could hardly believe my ears.

"Only our Pope can see Christ!"

"Which one? The blind one or the seeing one?"

"Our Holy Father, Juan Pablo Secundo!" The priest began to look away into the window.

I had no idea that a chocolate bar would start all this. I was determined to find out why the blind cardinal carried a stigmata of insanity and, what happened. Also, I had to consider the young priest's awkward position and had to be careful not to hurt his feelings of devotion toward hierarchy of the Catholic Church. Alberto gave me an encouraging twinkle in his eye and a more obvious push into my arm.

"Father, God is not a respecter of persons. Sun shines on everyone. Sometimes a blind person can see what a seeing one would not notice. Blindness can be a gift, so can a naiveté be a gift. Do you understand what I am saying?"

There was a moment of silence. The priest knew that I was waiting for an answer.

"Señora, this crazy cardinal went to Vatican to claim the office of Papacy. He said to our Holy Father that Christ has chosen him."

"That takes courage, don't you think?"

"A fool! Holy Father demanded an apology, but the fool would not take his claim back. So, he was excommunicated. Now he is on a crusade against our Holy Father."

"Courage of this kind comes from Spirit."

"Devil made him do it!" says the priest quickly and crosses himself, remaining in silence for a while.

I gave him all the time he needed to calm himself down. He was so young, about twenty-eight. His features were so lovely, his medium height body was dressed in a navy blue habit. He would make a perfect husband to some girl. So many women in South America dream about a man like him.

"Are you going to visit your family, Father?"

"Yes, I am going to baptize my new niece."

"How lovely. My four children were baptized in Chile too. The priest's name was Padre Salvador. What's your name, Father?"

"Raul. And what is yours, Señora?"

"Ingrid... Ingrid Heller!"

"A pleasure to meet you!"

I nodded my head and smiled at him. He felt at ease. A perfect moment to continue in our discussion.

"Have you heard of duality, Father Raul?"

"Duality? Like male and female, good and evil, Heaven and Hell?"

"Black and white, light and darkness, negative and positive...." I added.

"Yes. What are you trying to tell me, Sister?"

"That was excellent! You called me Sister, my Brother! One without the other doesn't have a meaning. There must be contrasts and opposites in everything. Their interplay leads to progress. It all comes from one Source - Unity. It is good for your Holy Father to have an opposition. This false Pope can teach him more than anyone else. Do you know what I mean, Brother Raul?"

I could see in his eyes that he was trying to understand, thinking about my words, wanting to say something but, words were missing. The clarity was not there.

"Brother Raul, we are One in the human family. All of us are sharing this Planet. We must be here for some reason. We are here to learn something, right?"

"Yes, to accept Jesus Christ as our Saviour."

"How do we go about it?"

"By praying, confessing our sins, repenting."

"Jesus was a good teacher and example. He always said: 'I am the way'. He never rejected anyone. He healed those who came to him to be healed and asked us to love each other the way He loved us. He taught us to love our enemies. He embraced the darkness by descending to Hell. It says in your Credo. He redeemed the World with all that there is, including the opposites........ Once we learn to understand our opposite, there is no more darkness and no more secrecy.

We need to seek Knowledge and Truth. At the beginning and at the end all is One. Only in the middle it is divided. Creation is perfect, Brother Raul!"

"Because our Father in Heaven is Perfect." Raul's eyes kept on following the silhouette of the Cordillera. He was at peace with himself and I was truly happy for him. I left him alone. Suddenly I hear a soft snore. It was Alberto's. I placed his new leather jacket over his shoulders and observed him for a while. As long as there was a ceasefire in our conversation, he followed with his mind. The later subject must had become boring to him. Frequently I wondered what kind of a woman would Alberto marry. There are more women per one man in South America, a true phenomenon. He might stay single, enjoying them all.

My mind had taken on its wings and I was back on Calle Ahumada, near Huérfanos, seeing my Priest-King, my christed one. Obviously, I must be crazy, by the Pope's standard. I was quite anxious to share the spiritual depth of my encounter with someone. Frankly, I wasn't even sure that my best friend Hanna would believe it. Despite her wisdom, she'd be sceptic. Probably my old friend Ray would be open to it. He is well read in esotericism. One person would be open to it: my friend Aaron! He is always neutral and gives the most sincere feedback. He comes from oneness. I was looking forward to my return to Santiago. Maybe I'll see my Priest again, if good luck would have it. I was contemplating on a trip to Concepción. Somehow I felt I should be there.

I must had fallen asleep. A gentle touch on my shoulder woke me up. It was Father Raul.

"Sister, I am very happy I have met you. I will always remember you."

I could feel a sorrow of parting again. I stood up and gave him a hug. He was open to it.

"May Peace be with you, Brother Raul...."

He is walking toward the front door, giving me one more look. He blushed slightly.

Alberto was awake, watching "chicas" boarding our bus.

"Señora, the priest is looking back here. He is waving to you! You must have impressed him!"

I waved back to Raul, who was already on another bus.

This stop was in Los Andes, the major crossroads. It was the town of the legendary Santa Teresa.

Alberto must had gotten tired of 'new chics', looking at my image in the window. It was very dark outside and the driver kept the dimmed lights on.

"You surely have a crush on Priests, don't you, Señora Ingrid!?" says Alberto.

"I like them innocent, Alberto, I like them innocent...."

Three hours later he transferred to the bus to his town. He thanked me for the trip, my company and the jacket. He said it all in an Argentinian accent.

I was going back to the hotel Libertador, planning the next few days. I didn't have much time left in this country. Married or not, I was determined to find out who my Priest was, if he was a priest.

Concepción

Instead of sitting in lotus position and meditating on the subject "Quest for Priest", to get his name, address and phone number, I searched in a dimension of time and space. Since it was the world I knew the best and my mind couldn't play tricks on me in the tangible reality, I felt totally comfortable about what I was doing. When Don Quijote de la Mancha found his sweetheart, his image of the perfect female was crushed. The image of my male was perfectly all right with me. He was handsome and attractive and I could describe his features at any time to anyone. Only I could not draw his image. Me, who used to do portraits, could not place his face on paper. A combination of nordic and jewish is hard to draw. His face, the masque, was so familiar, I began to question whether I've seen him in this lifetime somewhere after all.

Let's suppose that he is a priest. Patricia mentioned The Order of Santa Gemita. I inquired. No one of the described features was a part of the Chilean Santa Gemita group. The next step was the office of the archbishop. Apparently, the registry had no photographs of priests. I was afraid to talk about Jesus Christ's image. They might had told me that only John Paul II can look like that. The archbishop was out of town at a very important meeting. I figured they planned their strategy of how to overthrow the government. Junta members were regular at masses and probably generous in donations. Favours with God cannot be bought though, they have to be earned. When Church is bought, it can be bought by anyone. It cannot be trusted. There is always someone who plays the Almighty, anonymously.

My next destination was Concepción in the middle of Chile. I took with me Patricia's mother. Señora Rosa was a country woman with ladylike manners.

We arrived to Concepción on Friday, the 22nd of July, the Saint Magdalene's Day. The city is well known for its university surrounded by a lovely park and, for its leather and textiles.

We checked into a hotel, hired a taxi driver and went on. First, we shopped for wools. It had to be pure virgin. We found it in every store. We got a good deal in one of them.

In the morning someone slid a newspaper under our hotel room door. Señora Rosa picked it up and started to read.

"Señora Ingrid, the cardinal meets with the representatives of the Church here in Concepción today!"

"It sounds like a conception of something. Does it say where?"

"No, it does not!" answers Rosa sadly.

One hour later we asked our friendly taxi driver. He took us to the office of Alejandro Goic-Karmelic, the big boss of the church. His nun secretary had no information for us. The taxi driver was curious why we wanted to know about the meeting. We had to tell him some of the truth. He believed that one of the priests of the nearby Lotta matched the description. We went. On the way he pointed a location to us where a school bus had an accident and many children died. Since then, when anyone stops there, people hear voices of children calling for their family members. No one likes to stop there anymore.

Lotta was a small town where people heat their homes by burning coals and tires. It smelled bad. The parish had a mustard yellow colour. I walked in alone. An older priest of high stature received me. I asked for a younger one. He said they were working. When I asked him if any of the younger priests were in Santiago on July thirteenth, he became nervous. He denied it. It was obvious to me that he suspected I was some kind of agent. There was no way he would trust me. Then I had an idea.

"Father, I'd like to confess..."

"The mass is over, Señora Heller."

"But I sinned, Father!"

"Sorry, I cannot help you!" he answered calmly, walking me to the door.

I turned to him, giving him a note with our hotel's phone number and asked him if he could call me later. He said he had nothing to talk about.

He hopefully remembered my last words to him: "Father, be at peace. There is nothing to fear about me."

Obviously, I messed up. The taxi driver had another idea. He knew that Señor Goic-Karmelic was a kind and sensitive person, therefore, he believed if I'd write a letter to him, I might get some answer later on. I did that. The same lovely secretary promised to pass the letter to the Señor.

We were dropped off in the hotel and prepared for our return. We hoped to receive a phone call, but in vain.

We left Concepción the following morning and on the way encountered a very thick fog. The bus driver did a super job, being delayed only one hour.

My departure for Canada was coming closer and I accomplished hardly anything in my search. I decided to postpone my flight one week. I didn't contact all the people I wanted to be in touch with and yet, had more business to deal with.

Before returning to Santiago, I wanted to spend couple of days in the countryside where we lived upto four years ago. Señora Rosa made sure that one of their bedrooms was available to me. They used to be our neighbours and the walk from their place toward the land we owned was only fifteen minutes.

I was hoping for some revelation through the dream and prayed to be guided to the people who could assist me. I needed to open many doors and wait for the first indications of a successful search. Time mattered no more. I was prepared to give it all and had given conception to many ideas.

In Concepción on July 22nd, 1988

H o p e

Six years ago I had no idea why I moved to Chile and where it was eventually leading to. I believed in the South American continent and a Chilean future. Despite the present political situation, in my heart I knew that this was a country of hope.

The afternoon in the countryside was quite pleasant. My destination was my ex-residence with my ex-husband. The weather has been kind - the road was easy to walk. I looked ahead into Cordillera de la Costa and its highest peak. There were gold mines in the area, which perhaps explained frequent UFO sightings. Everyone had seen them few times at least.

I chose not to go into my memories. They were mostly painful. I kept on filling my lungs with the purity of country air, inhaling on the count of five, holding it upto ten and exhaling slowly. My walking pace slowed down. I was peaceful, grateful, joyous.

This country offered me a range of human experience I could not have anywhere else. What else was to happen? The future is fascinating when we don't know what it brings. And we have the power to create it! Human beings must be made well, since we can be trusted. We must be made in God's image and mind. We must be a well premeditated experiment. Do we really have a free will? If so, upto what point? And what happens after we complete with our and God's will? Do we go beyond that and become co-creators with God? What happens to the evolution of matter and spirit? Who is responsible for what? If the human being is entrusted with the blueprint of creation and evolution, then it is upto the human being to bridge action from one point to the other. A chain reaction, like Jacob's ladder. Only by winding stairs we can climb the tower. We cannot possibly envision the greatness of our mission, however small it may be.

I felt very loved and began to realize how important my little existence was and that there was only one like me. There was no duplicate of Ingrid Heller anywhere in the vast Universe. I had to learn to trust my inner guidance more and literally follow my heart. I had the most powerful tool - I was in love. I met my match. His blueprint and map to Kingdom had to be similar to mine, if not identical. Yet, his lifetime experiences had to be different from mine. We were independent from each other, but shared each other during our blessed encounter. What would happen if we got together on that day? Would we stay together? My body was ready for him! A man like him should have at least one copy of himself! I wished to be the mother of his offspring. My womb had to be blessed by this maculate conception of the seed that would carry information of future race progenitor. This thought was extremely attractive, but was burdened with the tremendous responsibility of finding and sedducing my Priest within the next few years. Many women of my age were over menopause. Could I be another Sarah, Elizabeth or Anne and conceive a child at old age? The thought of being old didn't feel right. I wanted to find my Adam soon. There was one thing I knew for sure: I had to take it step by step. The major event had already happened : I've met him. The next step is gathering information that would lead me to him. Or, shall I simply dismiss him from my mind and trust that he'll appear again? At this point I wouldn't dare to do that. I needed to nurture the action with my thoughts and feelings of love. Every time I rewound my tape of memory, I experienced the same exalted feeling I had when I met him. I kept on repeating it many times a day. He's been doing the same. I knew that. As a matter of fact, I was aware that it was me who had to find him. It wasn't his responsibility. If Eve started all the trouble leading into exile, it had to be Eve again to bring her Adam back to Eden. Descent into the world of duality must had been a painful experience of separation. Now we were ascending, coming into Unity. Naturally, I was to succeed in my search of my beloved and the Paradise we were promised. A new hermaphrodite, the balanced being in male and female polarities was to emerge. Exciting times, indeed!

Nothing could hold me too long in the countryside. I was anxious to return to Santiago and stir up some action before my departure. I visited with all my ex-neighbours who kept on asking about my family's return to Chile. I could only promise them a visit. The marriage to my Canadian husband did not allow me the freedom to move to another country again. Señora Rosa predicted my return based on my encounter and her family dared to prophesy much greater possibilities. We parted in a very cordial way.

Prior to leaving their humble country home, I went to their garden where a grotto with a sculpture of Virgin Mary was. I prayed Love Rosary beads once - not the catholic mysteries and the tiring repetition of Hail Mary. I liked the mantra of Love Rosary, keeping on rolling the beads between my fingers. Interestingly, Rosa's german shepherd dog, observing me from a distance, not once disturbed my meditation. She was a daughter of our Sheba.

I stayed in the same hotel - Libertador. This room was more comfortable and had a bath tub instead of a shower. I wanted to plan a strategy, but it didn't feel right.

I went for a walk into the Ahumada passage. Crowded again, as usual. The corner with Huérfanos (which means Orphans) seemed different this time. The Paradise was gone - my beloved was not there. I kept on walking and noticed a young charming man walking parallel to me. He smiled at me. I walked toward the cathedral and entered. He followed. Could this be a coincidence? I hope not another Priest! I disappeared behind a pillar inside the cathedral to see if he was following me. He waited by the entrance. I had to pass by him on the way out. He might be my messenger. I addressed him.

"What would you like to talk about, little brother?"

He was pleased and immediately responded:

"Do you have a little time for a coffee? I'd like to talk to you."

"What about, little brother?"

"Francisco! My name is Francisco."

He had a pleasant appearance. I felt very comfortable around him.

"My name is Ingrid!"

"German?"

"No, Canadian. But my background is partially German."

We entered a busy coffee shop nearby.

He kept on looking into my eyes and spelled out a question. "Are you married?"

"Yes, I am. How about you?"

"Single. Aren't you planning a divorce? I am very attracted to you." His words poured out at me.

I must had blushed. I remembered this line. It's always the same. I gave Francisco a meak smile in appreciation of his compliment.

"Francisco, you should have no problem finding yourself a wife. There are so many pretty girls in this country who are looking for a charmer like yourself. Be patient! The right one will come along!"

"But they're not spiritual!"

"What do you know? Walking into a church means absolutely nothing. Truly spiritual people seldom go to church," I assured him.

"You are truly spiritual, Ingrid. I can see it!"

I paused for a while. His eyes were still fixed into mine, but he also looked through me and around me.

"Francisco, you could be my son!" I introduced him to some of the truth. "You need a young woman who could give you children!"

Francisco still keeps on looking at me in the same way. He had eyes to see. Alberto's words would transcend themselves into a higher level in this case. Has my beloved Priest also had eyes to see?

I began to appreciate Francisco's presence and invited him for a supper to the hotel.

He came. We had a great conversation. He was a spiritual lad, loved Greek and romantic poets and had a healthy flow of thought - he was a natural philosopher in his early twenties. We agreed to see each other before my departure.

There were other people whom I wanted to meet. I followed on it. In this case I had the address. I was a total stranger to them, yet they welcomed me as if they knew me. Actually, I felt slightly intimidated by their special treatment. Their teenage son was a well known poet and the host of some television shows. I was naturally curious about his talent and also my role in his life. They shared some of their dreams in which I appeared to them. Dreams are mostly genuine guidance once we work with them. I chose to leave some space for doubt. During the course of our absolutely magnificent conversation, I had to acknowledge that there was some special ingredient that produced a sweet sensation in our bodies. At times we could all see a white fog in the room of their house. We formed a circle, holding hands, and thanked the Creator for our special time together.

Then the mother of the young man went to look for something and returned with a flat black velvet box. She told me it was for me. I opened it. In it was a golden key about eleven centimetres long and a small tablet with an engraved dedication from a television network for the participation in their programmes during 1982. The key was to the door of the Catholic University in Santiago.

Diplomatically, I attempted to give them this precious gift back. It was their son's and not many people received this award. They all insisted I must accept it. I had no choice. When I asked why this gift, the boy's mother explained to me what preceded:

"Sister Ingrid, I felt that I had to give you something to remember us by, and went into my son's room. Thinking of what it should be, this box falls off the top shelf of my son's bookcase onto my head. It is a gift for you. You must accept it. This key is for you, not for my son!"

I gratefully accepted, but more like I felt as a custodian of this reward and decided to return the gift to them at some point of time in the future.

We were naturally curious about each other, exchanging information for several hours. They believed I had some mission in Chile and when I told them about my encounter with my Priest, they immediately thought of a priest from the Schønstat Brotherhood who had the qualities I described. This priest's name was Father Christian and he spent a lot of time with their son.

I met with the young poet's family two more times before my departure.

The following day I went to the Schønstat retreat that was located in the Florida district of Santiago. Father Christian was transferred to Ecuador, I was told. If he visited Santiago, he would call his Brothers.

I left crying, counting days. I had only three days left. Then I realized that during that time I could accomplish the impossible, meet new messengers, have a revealing dream, speak to gods. Only I had to remind myself not to lose the hope and faith in the perfect order of events.

Santiago is the name for St. James, the apostle of Hope. He was the brother of Christ, part of his inner circle, together with Peter and John. I've met my beloved in the perfect place on the perfect day in the country shaped as a sword.

The Andes are considered to be the spine of the planet, with Tierra del Fuego at its base and the turbulent Straits of Magallanes. Volcanic activity and earthquakes became a part of Chilean life.

Those who are seeking enlightenment would connect easily to my stream of thought regarding kundalini, chakras, sexuality, and love. The force has to be liberated, just like the consciousness of South American people. Did they hold the key to planetary liberation? Wouldn't that explain the social, economic and political struggle they are going through?

It was time to leave. The night before my flight we had a few tremblers. I became used to small earthquakes. Once in 1984 I was in the epicenter of about 6.0 on Richter scale. A vibrational force from the earth continued along my spine and exited through the top of my head. I was standing at that time. I kind of liked it. My children were calm about it too.

No person at the airport crowd would've reminded me of my Priest. I got a seat by the window. After the take off I looked into darkness with street lights of this enormous city of four and a half milllion. I left behind the deepest of human experiences that connected me eternally to this country. I had to come back! I could not imagine leaving for good. Yes, there is a time when I'll come back, or, at least, I had a Hope.

Together with the children back home on July 31st, l988.
From the left: Jean, Maria, Monica, Ingrid, Andrew, Joe..

R e c o r d s

My family was waiting for me at the airport. How precious are our children! Andrew and Maria asked immediately about the gifts I promised them. Joe gave me a sweet hug. He used to worry about me each time I went to give a childbirth. Jean was as usual - absolutely stable and detached. Monica welcomed me back and passed me the house key with the words "Mom, please, take over again!" Verne was all dressed up, as he used to be for our dates of dancing and laughter. He allowed the children time and space with me, observing me all the time.

It was his turn to greet me. No hug, no kiss. His words penetrated through my bones: "You've changed, Ingrid!" He was worried. I could see it.

"I know I've changed. I need three weeks to ground myself and all will be as before. Give me time."

"I would rather lose you to ten men than to this one!" he replied and said nothing since then on the way home.

I wondered how much he did know. Did he have some revealing dream, or sensed the change? Was I really so different that he assumed I must had fallen in love with someone else? Verne was a quite intuitive man. I didn't give him any sound reason about my delayed return, except phoned him that I'll be one week late. I had to become watchful over my thoughts. Telepathy is a natural phenomenon among family members. No one was supposed to know about the encounter. My friend Hanna and Ray would tell no one. They could be trusted. Frankly, I was anxious to tell them about my trip.

The family evening was nurturing. Children did well while I was away. Joe worked with Verne on most of days and Monica kept the household running efficiently. She is only eighteen years old. Four year old Andrew keeps the most in company of his two years older sister Maria. Thirteen year old Jean is independent. She likes to read, play piano and she probably helped Monica with chores. The vegetable garden was looked after well. Joe told me about his summer job with great pride.

Everyone liked the gifts I bought them. Verne admired the craftsmanship on the leather jacket. We felt peaceful together. I described to the children the changes in our past neighbourhood of the Chilean countryside. They were sad to hear about Sheba's death. Most of my pictures were developed in Santiago. The children recognized everyone and were happy to hear that nobody forgot them.

Verne fortunately didn't insist on intimacy. In two days he was to leave for a long trucking trip to U.S.A. Joe was to stay with us. He needed a vacation. The fourteen year old that looks like a child needs to sleep in sometimes.

Hanna wasn't home the following day either. She probably went camping with her five children. Ray was home. He was very happy to hear from me. His first question was about my fear of death I had prior to my trip. I told him about the encounter.

His reply was a simple question. "What will you do when you'll find your Priest?"

I had no answer.

He stated that I wasn't ready for him yet, but promised me that he'll try to get some information for me in meditation. Since I've known Ray for the last ten years, he's been doing the same thing: meditating many hours a day and keeping records of all his experiences. I never asked what his experiences were about, but he said he was working with angels. He was very particular about the secrecy. During his life of sixty-two years he never married or dated. He was introduced to me by a mutual friend, who was an inventor. Ray had some good feedback for me in the past. On occasions it was out of this world. He had absolutely no idea what a family life or a marriage was all about. He had difficulty understanding the realistic aspects of relationships. He admired writings of Rudolf Steiner and actually, thanks to Ray's influence, I somehow got involved in antroposophical movement and discussed various issues with him. He liked that. When I visited Goetheannum in Dornach near Basel, I could appreciate the greatness of Rudolf Steiner's work. That place is a living testimony itself, revealing the Mystery of mysteries: the Holy Grail mystery. One of Rudolf Steiner's incarnations was that of St. Thomas Aquinas. That was his personal claim.

I phoned my friend Aaron for an appointment. He was a well known Akasha reader and helped me in the past. Aaron is not a fortune teller. As a matter of fact, he never talks about the future. He talks about the present and its relationship to the past lives. He helped thousands to understand themselves and those around them better.

Aaron's office is very bright. Decor includes plants, paintings, symbols. There was always a bit of fragrance.

He was happy to see me and gave me one of his great hugs. He couldn't stop smiling. Did he notice something?

"You've changed, Ingrid.... you've grown...... your trip was a gift to your life. I am very happy for you!...Any questions?"

"Aaron, I met this man on July 13th right in the heart of Santiago. We experienced a rapture together that lasted several seconds and during that time he transmitted information to me about the two of us. I walked away from him because of my marriage, but later I regretted it. I want to find him again. I need help, Aaron. Can you collaborate on it, please?"

While I was speaking, Aaron closed his eyes. He breathed a few times deeply through his nose and hummed in a high pitch for a while. After a few more breaths he began to read from the Record of my Soul. "What we see here is a pattern of heresy in the late thirteen hundreds. He was a teacher in the movement of Rosicrucianism and you were one of the students. He admired your wisdom and made you an equal partner in teachings and then in life. Your gift was that of healing. You healed many and people came to you from far away. It worried your partner because the Church began to inquire about you. Eventually, he used this opportunity to challenge the Church about their healings. As a result of that you were burnt at the stake. He still feels guilty about it. He wants to be protective of you this time and doesn't want to involve you in his stream of life activity. He'd rather stay away from you than lose you...... In other lives you were his inspiration. Many times he was with someone else but loved you. You always got together at the most important times of history. You also died together a few times."

I was silent for a while, feeling the echo of Aaron's words that resonated inside me. He was telling me the truth.

"Is he a priest?" I asked.

"He cares about people, speaks on behalf of the oppressed. There were many missing in South America. He is involved with that movement. He keeps some records."

"Where is he, Aaron?"

"He is from around there."

"How will I find him, Aaron?"

"You've already found him. Through those eyes you established an eternal connection. He recognized you."

"Does he want me to find him again?"

"He has work to do. A family life would be in the way. Humanity is his family. Look, Ingrid, you have young children, a husband who loves you. That is your life now! That is your job. Let the other man go. Set him free! Do that for him and for yourself..... "

Aaron looked at me with gentle kindness. At this point I wasn't ready to hear what he was saying. I understood the importance of detachment and preferred to be that way, but I wanted to find my Priest again. What if he needs me? I might be able to help him with his work! What if he gets ill and has no one to take care of him? Regardless of reading, I had to find out on my own who my Priest was. I didn't want to tell Aaron all the details about our encounter. It was far too sacred to me. As I wouldn't tell anyone about my special spiritual experiences. I had to keep pearls to myself.

"I am proud of you, Ingrid, that you conquered your fear of dying and went on the trip anyway."

"I think I died on that street when I parted from him. We both died."

"Dying is a part of living. If you want to learn how to live fully, you have to learn how to die first. Every day you should repeat this process. That's what the carrying of the cross is all about. Some complain and pity themselves. Let them be then, walking in the same circle, getting nowhere. Crucifixion is for the kings, for the best of the crop."

Aaron pauses for a while and gives me time to contemplate on what he just said to me. "Since I've known you, Ingrid, you never complained about your hardships. Each time you come to see me, you are stronger, enriched. You always manage to transform the present situation into a higher one. You are always one step ahead of yourself. You have a power in your name. Heller, the one of the light, the one with halo. Ingrid is another. INRI was engraved on the cross!"

"Doesn't it mean 'Jesus of Nazareth, the King of Israel'?" I asked quickly.

"That is an explanation of the uninitiated ones. It has much greater significance. It is the secret to alchemy, the old hermetic science of transmutation. Seek, and you shall find. You are an alchemist already."

"What is the most important message you would have for me right now, Aaron?"

"Your throat has to be developed. I can hear you singing with much greater power. Will you sing again?"

"I am considering auditioning for the Bach Chamber Choir. I love baroque music."

"You were a boy soprano at that time. You actually knew Johann Sebastian Bach in person. I wouldn't be surprised that his music will open another door for you. Keep on singing, heal the constriction in your throat. Liberate the speech, so wisdom can be expressed in words."

"Is my Priest a singer too?"

"He might be. He is Logos, a powerful speaker! But don't worry about him. You are to focus on yourself."

Aaron gave me more information about my children and our relationships. It was very interesting and I could relate to that. The reading and hour was over. The whole session was taped and I could hardly wait to listen to it again at home when I have some private time.

It is easy to part with forty year old Aaron. He is so detached and neutral. Not once I felt from him a judgement or any unpleasant emotion. He loves his work and he is very good at it.

Hanna came back from her vacation. She was so anxious to hear about my trip, she rushed over to my place the following day to hear Aaron's reading, see photographs from Chile and to see me. I was still in that radiant state and my body felt pregnant.

The children were busy playing together. Hanna has five children, but brought with her only the three youngest ones, who are very compatible in ages with Maria and Andrew.

We both listened attentively to the tape and discussed many possibilities. Hanna was excited about my trip experience and helped with a good suggestion."Why do you believe that he was a visitor? In Chile there are immigrants from many countries. The German and Jewish communities must be strong. Your ex-husband might know about him. Ask him. We always come back to the same conclusion: the world is small."

"I just remember, Hanna. My "ex" went to a private school founded and operated by Belgian priests in the area of Providencia, which is next to downtown. I am going to phone him tonight about it. Hey, thanks!"

"Remember, there is always a solution to every problem we're facing. Life is never hard on us. Things happen because we are ready for them."

"I agree, Hanna. Life is continuously directing us into a progress and transcendence of our own nature."

We chatted about many other subjects, mostly related to our children. Later on in the afternoon we took the children to a large playground in my district. It faced west with the magnificent Rockies and we could observe the calm flow of the Bow River in the valley below. When the children got tired of swinging, Hanna and I took over and enjoyed the exciting feeling rushing up our spine, bringing the memories of childhood, nurturing the child within.

Later on that night I phoned my Chilean ex-husband Eduardo, asking him about the teachers in the Notre Dame School. I described the features of my Priest and received an answer that astonished me. The founding priest was of a very high stature, but passed away in recent years. There was another one, also tall, who taught French and Religion, who looked very much like my Priest, according to my description. I asked more about him. I could identify many resemblances. That same night I wrote a letter to the school with a request for Father Jacob's address. I mailed it registered the next day.

During the same week I obtained a card from Concepción from Señor Alejandro Goic-Karmelic with Padre Christian's address to Ecuador. I was thrilled! One more person believes that I've met Father Christian. I wrote him a letter on the same day, mentioning the time of my encounter with a brief description of what happened. I wrote nothing about the Christ image. I asked Father Christian to answer me if there was any connection with him. I also sent this letter by registered mail.

Hanna and I kept on phoning each other daily. She became involved in my search very deeply and sometimes had a dream for me. Nothing led into an answer. Ray became critical toward my search. He openly told me that if I find my "man" soon, we'll likely end up in bed and will never want to see each other again. He felt it would be better never to find him and rather keep the romance on a higher level, without any physical contact.

50

What did Ray know about love, anyway? He obviously spoke from his own experience that must had been very basic. Would this explain his ascetic life denying his own sexuality? A suppressed sexuality is a suppressed expression of the life force, the healing and creative energy that evenually leads to genius in a human being. Now I was clearer on the meaning of "master bed", or the "lectus genialis". If Ray's opinion would be right, Romans would call the bed "lectus genitalis" and the English would call it "mastur bate". I considered Ray just a little challenge.

V i r g o - The Seventh Month

The children were absolutely fantastic the whole summer. Many times we went to the playground above the river valley, where I felt so free in my childlike dreaming, thinking of fairy tales, about the magical kiss of pure love that interrupted a deep sleep and everyone became alive in the kingdom again..

One early afternoon the door bell rang. I could see through the glass door that it was the mailman. He had a registered letter for me from Ecuador. I perspired while signing for it. My hands turned cold and I was actually trembling. I rushed into the kitchen to open it. I read the well spread handwriting::

Señora Ingrid! I was very pleased to read about your experience in Santiago. I have never seen an angel myself, but firmly believe that some of them live among us. At the time of your encounter I was in Ecuador. I pray that you will find what you are looking for. You may maintain in correspondence with me, if you wish. I keep very busy with my work, but am able to find some time for myself. Blessings! Father Christian.

A wave of cold swept over me. One door of hope had to be closed. I am holding Christian's letter, breathing its fragrance. I also keep paper for writing to special people in a box with fragrance. His frangrance was musk, emanating a masculine energy. I thanked him for his answer on the feminine rose scented paper.

We kept in written contact for all these years. Later, it narrowed to a Christmas card, but Christian held a balance for me that I needed so much at that time. There will be a day when the two of us will meet and I'll thank him personally for his sensitivity and kindness. I had no answer from the Notre Dame School. No news is good news - I had a hope. Many times a day I repeated the encounter in my mind and it kept on intensifying the energy. Was Father Christian suggesting that I might had seen an angel? When I thought about it more, I was indeed looking at my Priest with a child like wonder, which I experienced in my early childhood when on St. Nicolas' Day my parents hired actors from the theater in angel's, devil's and St. Nicolas' costumes. I've met a supernatural beings. My attention was focused entirely on the angel and St. Nicolas. These were powerful moments. I was only two at that time. Two years later, when I already sinned a little, all my attention went to the devil, whose costume was so complete, that he had actual hoofs, horns, tail, and a chain. My brother and I were so frightened that we promised obedience and prayed to our guardian angel.

Music was my daily remedy. I either listened to some, or played some. Knowing about the power of the sound and music, I hoped to be able to communicate to my Priest through my song. OMBRA MAI FU from Handel's Xerxes became a means of communication. My heart and throat sang for my Priest. I also sang Bach's Ave Maria. Catholic archetypes never bothered me. The mind works with pictures and visualization. The universe works with sound. I nurtured my imagery and sent the vibrational waves of my own voice to him, whom I loved.

The days were adding up. The children started school. Verne left for another trucking trip. We still avoided intimacy. I began to wonder whether he respected my wishes or if we were creating a gap between the two of us. I had to be truthful in my relationship. Sometimes I felt sorry for my husband. He was kind, worked hard and seldom complained. I felt like betraying him. I had to make a choice. I chose my marriage. It was the reality of time. We had a short honeymoon again, until I was kissed by true love. All this happened in the month of the Virgin, the maiden of the harvest.

The early morning of September 12th 1988 I was kissed again by my husband on my right cheek. It was a loving ritual, practiced by him faithfully since we've been together. He never woke me up in the mornings, he quietly got up on his own and got ready for work. This morning was as usual. After the kiss he wished me and the kids a lovely day and left. I woke up, scan the room with my eyes, check the clock. It was six in the morning. Another hour of sleep before a busy day starts. I was trying to go back to sleep, but all of a sudden, I was standing on the cobble stone street, looking around to identify the location. There were people around me I could not see. I just felt them and heard them. They spoke a different language - it sounded germanic. The place was quite warm on this sunny day. There was a church at my far left and a few meters in front of me was a water canal with some small boats. Along both sides of the canal there was a lane of trees. The bridge at my left and at my right led to the other side of the canal next to which there was another pathway. All this time my eyes were focused on the houses attached to each other that were on the pathway across the canal. I could smell flowers everywhere. I heard the sound of bicycles, tramways and I could hear the boats' whistles in a nearby harbour. I could smell the sea. I was getting used to brightness and was looking into a blue sky. I saw a large white bird, whose wings spread about two meters, gliding across the sky at my right. He saw me. It was my Priest! I hear the crowd exclaiming in admiration "LOOK AT THAT BIRD!" He flew toward me and attempted to land. I was kissed by him on my right cheek! It was magical! Then he landed in front of me on the balancing beam made of the red oak tree. The shape of the beam was carved by hand. One second later the bird descended off the beam and positioned himself on the opposite side of it. I was overwhelmed by his presence and stretched my right hand to caress him. His soft white feathers felt warm. I touched his back and proceeded along the neck toward his head. His eyes looked into mine so lovingly, radiating devotion. I must had pleased him with my touch, because he joyfully and rapidly rose over my head, forming prolonged circle of his flight, directly into the blue sky. I lost the sight of him when he was merging with the sun. I was blinded by its brightness. He appeared again and flew toward me. His color had changed into a dark green and his body became very thin. He kissed me again on my right cheek, showering me with love I had never known before. It was intimate and pure. When he completed the oval loop, he passed in front of my face, and changed again into a bird looking more like a phoenix, with only emerald and indigo colours in his plumage. He opened two pairs of wings. I heard the crowd exclaiming in awe "LOOK AT THOSE COLOURS!" The bird ascended energetically into the blue sky. His wings merged together into a ring around his body and he assumed the form of Saturn. The joy I felt was ineffable. I was still standing on the street, feeling its stones under my feet. Where was I? I touched my right cheek, feeling the vibrations of the kisses. I placed my hand where true love had kissed me.

I was in my bed again, ecstatic with joy. Where is my love? Does he live in those houses?

What a gift this was for my upcoming forty second birthday! I added another blessing to my life and thanked the Creator for everything that led to this moment.

There was no way that Hanna would not be notified about my experience. She asked me a few smart questions to make sure that my husband's kiss could not be mistaken with the bird's kiss. The difference was remarkable in intensity and chronology. We made guesses about the bird and the location. The closest we came to was a heron and any city in the Low Countries that had water canals. We thought of Amsterdam and Brugge, yet neither of us visited these cities. I just passed through Amsterdam once on the way from Schiphol airport to Centraal Station to get to Paris.

I phoned Aaron about my "dream". He was very happy about it and suggested that the bird represented nobility and that the set of double wings signifies the flight of time through this three dimensional world. When I told him that I must find the exact location, or, I'll never have peace, he encouraged me very vaguely. He thought it wasn't necessary. For the first time I stopped trusting him. I felt that for some strange reason he was actually discouraging me and I could not understand his motivation. I knew he wanted me to work on my marriage instead. Aaron was a firm believer in the NOW. Whatever we have in our life at the given moment is there to teach us something, and we are to seek a perfect relationship in any given situation. He said that we have no relationship with anyone except ourselves and that we are only learning how to relate.

Aaron had a message for me. About one week later I decided to work on my marriage and create the dream I had prior to my wedding. It was about time to bring some realistic sense to my daily existence and create a harmony and balance.

We were entering the sign of Libra, the sign of balance, and the month number eight. The energy flow within the figure eight is self regenerating, running on its own power. It is clearing and purifying.

Promise

All was back to normal. Every day had about the same routine. It felt comfortable. I put out the garden, raked the leaves, cleaned the windows and waited for the winter with the longest night of the year.

Verne and I went to Octoberfest again, where we met two years ago. We danced with each other the whole night. I paid attention only to him and watched so he wouldn't go into his crisis of jealousy and insecurity. It seemed to be his weakness in the past.

All went well and we entwined again.

A couple of nights later, during an early morning hour, I was half awake, feeling the freshness of the wind. Our window was slightly open. I thought the wind was coming through the window when, suddenly, in front of me I saw my Priest walking toward me with his arms stretched out in receiving. He wore a dark tunic that was ankle length. The western wind blew against him, trying to stop his movement. I noticed he walked on the stormy water. He calls out to me "Promise me you will keep on searching for me! Promise that you'll find me! Promise!"

I promised....,.and was trying to reach his hands, attempting to take him out of the water and onto the shore. I was stretching my arms out, but could not reach him. There was a space between us. My heart was torn. I felt his desperation and his cry for help.

Nothing was the same in my marriage anymore. The honeymoon was brief. That same day I took off my wedding band and placed it under a lamp on the night table next to our bed. Our bed was an antique bed and was neither a king or queen size, but a double bed.

I prayed for help and answers and looked for literature that would help me understand what I was going through. There is a saying that life starts at forty two. Where was my start, since all effect is the result of a cause? Then again, I was the creator of my present situation, the actor on the stage, trying to remember what the next line was. With all the tools I was given at the time of my conception, creating every cell of mine, creating a temple to house my spirit, those same tools had to assist me now. In my essence there was encoded information for which I needed a key. I had been given a key to the Catholic University. Which door should I open? At times I hesitated to accept messages literally. There is more than one meaning to everything. It escalates. As above, so is below. Somehow, somewhat, I had to get to the next line of my comedy. It wasn't even funny anymore. But life consists of ups and downs. We soar to heights as an eagle, and between we creep in the lowest, hiding ourselves in the sands of the desert, crawling backwards, just like scorpions.

Libra was over and the challenge of the Scorpio energy presented itself very clearly. The ninth month. The first power of three. It can either expand itself into the second power of eighty one, or consume itself. Was I anxious and pushing too hard to fly among eagles, perhaps? If we are at peace with ourselves, we can connect to the universal mind which is omnipotent, omnipresent and omniscient.

I needed some good humour again to allow myself to recuperate from my seriousness. The quest of ourselves cannot afford a heaviness. I've seen far too many serious spiritual seekers, the martyrs, judgemental toward anyone who dared to have some fun. I was going to challenge it. God must have a sense of humour! How could he otherwise create this universe with laughter in it?

Verne and I were going to go to the Hallowe'en dance. We had to be original. I found black satin pants that had a leather look, and a black top that suited the fabric. Verne had a black turtleneck and slacks. With a help of some silver glitter chains, some red, and a few stars for our faces, we became Mister and Miss Universe. Everybody read us at the dance. I had on both sleeves in silver glitter written MISS UNIVERSE and on the back I broke it into MISS-UNI-VER-SE. Over my breast I had in the same silver the MILKY WAY and right under my belly in the red glitter the BLACK HØLE, with the O crossed like a stop sign. And those who read my buttocks had more to laugh about. I placed on one half a silver moon crescent to moon the world and on the other half I placed a constellation of the BIG DIPPER, with the literal explanation. My husband was a perfect match with MR. UNIVERSE on his sleeves and on his back, yet over his chest he had written in the same silver glitter OMNIPOTENT and from that point straight down into his groin area he wore a long tie that was getting wider toward the lower point, with gradually enlarged letters saying EXPANDINK. The last four letters fitted right over the private area. We were nominated by most of people as the best costumes.

The celebration of the night transformed itself at midnight to enter the All Saints Day. Black and White, always in the company of each other. The balance was back. The challenge of the Scorpio is the transformation and transcendence.

Even Hanna noticed that I was more peaceful again. I allowed the natural flow to help me in my search. If I were to stay with Verne, it would happen. Outwardly I was supportive of my marriage, inwardly I was seeking my true love. I read somewhere that we love one man through many men. Therefore, the ultimate relationship exists, but we must be ready for it so it would manifest. I had to prepare for the ultimate.

There was no answer from the Notre Dame School. I was in the stalemate. Some days it bothered me. Those days I sang Ombra Mai Fu again. In the middle of November another gift came my way.

Toward the morning I heard in my left ear a name repeated twice. A pleasant man's voice is giving me this name. It was very familiar and I felt that the first name resembled a Czech name Jarek, but it sounded more like Yariek. The surname had ended with "man" and the word "library" came through. I had perceived in my mind a phone line giving me this name. I stood in front of a gothic arch shaped door and pressed a doorbell. A tall partially bald DOORMAN in a preacher's outfit opens. I said that Yariek wanted to speak with me. I heard a resonant man's voice coming from the left saying: "Tell her I'll speak with her when I am done!" The preacher told me that Yariek was very busy. Instead of being at the door entrance now, I was standing on the sandy path leading to the stone ascending stairway. The word SENDERO flashes in my mind.

I added this dream to my journal. I knew I was given another key and had to figure out its meaning.

I remembered the energy of Yariek from one special experience I was awarded on Mother's Day in the year 1980, soon after I married Eduardo. At that time Yariek was an overseeing teacher, being pleased with my progress. It happened in a location that actually exists, yet, my experience took place on the etheric plane. It was a large cathedral dedicated to Mary and besides it there was a grotto. I knew the exact interior, including paintings of angels and clouds on the high ceiling above the unusual altar that had a shape of a wooden large desk. Where was it?

Before my father died, he took my brother and I to the puppet theater occasionally and bought us a couple of puppets representing Father and Son. Their names were Spejbl and Hurvínek We played puppets and created a script right on the spot. I had a special feeling for my puppet with the identity of a puppeteer. All that puppet had to do was surrender. I trusted the process already in progress to do the same. I surrendered. I felt an irresistable impulse to look into a box with souvenirs from my European honeymoon. The next thing I knew I was holding a pamphlet in my hand, which I picked up in the church of St. Germain-au-Près in Paris. The bronze eagle bible stand near the entrance inside this church made a powerful impression on me. There were many pamphlets in the church available to choose from. I picked only one about the pilgrimage to Lourdes. After reading it now, I look up some information about the location in a Encyclopaedia Britannica. It was the same cathedral! Was I to return to Europe and find answers there? We were entering Sagittarius - the Archer. My aim was my native continent for completion of number ten - December.

A d a m   a n d   E v e

Decembers in my city can be either very cold, or quite pleasant. It depends on the direction of the wind. The daily transportation of the children to and from school, plus the care of Andrew, household, and the yard kept me very busy. I was looking forward to our first family Christmas with Verne.

The preparations can be exciting. We bought many beautiful decorations and chains and made a ritual of decorating the tree. I placed my favourites in the center. It was a dove and the Star of David. Some call it the Seal of Solomon.

Christmas music was played at all times in our house. Whenever I had a moment, I practiced singing for the Christmas concert of the Bach Choir. The major part of the program was "Jesu Meine Freude", meaning "Jesus, my Master". It is a very devotional piece.

Our concert went very well. Verne didn't show up. I noticed that he was not thrilled about my involvement with the choir. Verne was by birth Sagittarius, just like my both parents and my daughter Monica. I learned not to challenge any of them. It can result in a volcanic eruption. They're Fire. And on top of it, I had an ascendant Sagittarius at the time of my birth. I never was a typical Virgo.

This was the first time since my first marriage that I could plan Christmas shopping without worrying. It felt great! I was responsible with the money and included practical gifts. Maria and Andrew still believed in Santa Claus, Jean made me believe that she did. Monica helped with gift wrapping and some Christmas baking. It looked like a perfect festive season on the outside. Inside I was longing for the union with my beloved and hoped for some miracle, or a sign.

In the evenings, before I retired, I retreated into the living room by the Christmas tree, allowing myself the luxury of daydreaming, giving wings to my thoughts.

The blinking of colourful Christmas lights almost hypnotized me. I used the Star of David as a gateway, while playing music by a Chilean composer Joakín Bello that my Chilean friends sent me for Christmas. I was again endulging in the piece called Andesenios. It starts with a water fountain introducing Tibetan music and blends into a Gregorian chant sang by well selected male voices, being overlapped by angelic voices. The last lines of devotionally repeated "Gracia Criste" ended in electronic sounds with a soundtrack of birds and a puma.

In moments of devotion we become truly intimate with ourselves, when nothing else really matters. I can understand the subtle passion of the monk. Expressing love toward a human being is somehow different from the love we feel toward our Creator, unless, we recognize the divine essence in the human being. Only then our love becomes divine and we revere all life. Once we taste the sweetness of that perfect love, we are willing to do anything to feel it again. For that love people made superhuman tasks and by their action left us a statement that life without a true love has no meaning. Everyone seeks completion and union, whatever their consciousness is. Some express it in their promiscuous nature, some fight the battles, some write and compose, some die for it. The Christ child within, the christic consciousness is a fruit of that perfect union of Alpha and Omega.

In my native Bohemia we celebrate the birth of Christ on the twenty fourth of December. It is the day of Adam and Eve, the day to celebrate their oneness before the Exile from the Garden of Eden, or, their return to Eden. The Seal of Solomon, the Star of David, represents that perfect union.

Everyone was happy about the gifts. Everyone, but Verne. He complimented on my smart shopping and the next day he asked me how I paid for it. I told him the truth. Some cash, some with credit card. When I took the children skiing during the school break, we had to return home. The credit card was cancelled. It explained why Verne didn't want to join us. We had an argument. My peace was taken from me. I grieved. Every year I was reminded that Christmas is an intense time. It reminds us of who we are and what side of life we represent. Verne was on the opposite side of mine. I was not upset about it. I was going to grow faster next to him. We still shared the same bed but made no love. Him and I could not enter a dimension of Paradise together.

I became an observer of my own act in action. Obviously, this marriage was coming to completion. It was clear to me when Verne asked me for a divorce. I asked him to reconsider and to be less rational. We became a couple again just for a short while. It didn't feel right. There was no presence of devotion or love for each other. Yet, I was grateful that he was in my life. He assisted me in meeting my beloved and helped me with the children for a while. I couldn't help the feeling that he completed something he owed me from the past. Aaron did a reading for us once. He said it himself that our relationship was strictly karmic. Without Verne's help I wouldn't be able to travel to Santiago and be generous with my friends. Verne held a very special post in my life. Now, he was willing to step down and allow me the freedom to find my path to Eden so at the end of cycle I could partake of the Fruit of the Tree of Life and share it with my Adam.

Prayer of the Virgin

Doubtlessly, there was an intense time ahead. More patience and strength was needed. Every day had some surprise for me. The festive season was over and we parted with our Christmas tree. I placed the Star of David into a separate box with other special objects that were meaningful to me. Among them was a Rosary that was given to me for Christmas in 1981 in Chile. I took out a note with Love Rosary and found a comfort I needed praying it, running beads between my fingers. It became my daily ritual before falling asleep.

Exactly on the last day of January 1989, from the prayer I was taken into a room that had three objects on the wall, all of them made of ceramic, except the one in the middle. The object on the left side was in the shape of a three story brown house with a large ribbon at the base saying ANTWERPEN. The middle object was an oval mirror in the golden antique frame. On the right side there was a brown cross with a male figure hanging upside down. I smelled a fragrance, but couldn't recognize its origin. The walls in the room were of peach colour. I wrote about the experience in my journal. It was an unusual message indicating that I had my answers in Belgium in Antwerp.

I sent a letter to my friends in Santiago asking them to speak with the director of the Notre Dame School about my request for Father Jacob's address. At this time the schools had summer holidays. I had to wait for an answer for almost two months.

Ray phoned me about a dream he had. He said that my Priest was in turmoil not knowing how to find me. He also said that I had a better chance of finding him.

This information didn't help. It stressed more responsibility on me and I ached again. My prayers to Divine Mother became a frequent necessity. I needed more than strength. I asked for a direction to the next step.

Within one week another important dream came through: I am walking in a European city on the sidewalk, looking at numbers of houses. All these houses were attached to each other. One entrance door was open. I enter and sit down in a waiting room with antique furniture arranged in a cozy way. I observe wall hangings. Paintings were of Flemish landscapes. I could see through a glass door with fine lace curtain into a next room. There were two men in conversation. The blond man leaves and the other tall man asks me in. He knows my name. He wore a black tunic. I am asked to sit at his desk and he shifts his chair close to mine. He is about my age, dark hair, very handsome features. Our eyes keep communicating. It was extremely loving and sweet. His blue eyes were deep and pure. Everything about him was very spiritual. He passes me a white envelope in which I find a vial with a white powder and a hand written note saying that I was to use the substance of alchemy. The note was signed by the writer. He is known as an Alchemist. I cannot reveal his name. I was filled with gratitude. My friend nods in agreement with the note, rises and leads me to the door. The blond friend, whose name was Josef, is coming back. Out of the door, into a street and ...,.I am back in my bed.

The city I was in was unknown to me, yet, the personality was someone very familiar. The time will tell.

In March I received a phone call from Santiago. My friends had the address of Father Jacob. They dictated it to me. It was to a parish in Deurne in Belgium. I chose a post card with the beautiful Lake Louise and wrote to Father Jacob that I had a story to tell him and also that I had the key to Iannua Coeli. I included my address and mailed it on the same day.

Good News

There was a tension in our home in the evenings. Verne kept more to himself and spent less time with the children. Our double bed became a single bed overnight - I began to sleep on the sofa in the living room. Verne stopped talking about a divorce when I told him that I will not oppose it if he petitions. He didn't come to Monica's graduation either. Everything was just a matter of time.

In the beginning of May a Petition for a Divorce was served to me and I had to learn in a hurry how to answer it on my own. I could not afford a lawyer. Clerks in the court house were the most helpful. I had nothing to ask of the marriage, no child custody was involved. Our case was simple. The children were calm because I was calm. There was no animosity. They liked Verne, but he was in their life for a too short time. Monica was concerned about our survival. She was graduating and wanted to go to a Bible College that was in Swift Current in Saskatchewan. I would rather have her in the city studying for a more practical career. She had already decided. Luckily, she was offered a loan that she accepted. She encouraged me about my possible future work, suggesting interpreting, translating, marketing, sewing, and babysitting. Yes, there were many decisions to be made.

At all times my mind had to be clear and calm. I had to find a way into the future, willing to consider all opportunities A few days after I was served a petition, I received a short letter from Father Jacob from Belgium.. He was very curious how I knew about him and expressed a desire to hear about the story I had for him. He answered me in Spanish but mentioned that he was French speaking. He was not in the parish in Deurne for the last four years, yet, my card was forwarded to him. He resided in Antwerp. My hopes were high!

I phoned Hanna immediately and she was very excited about it. We talked like a two teenage girls, fantasizing all the possible outcomes. Ray was informed as well, except, he was not too happy about it. It really surprised me.

I answered Jacob's letter within a couple of days. I was very particular about proper spelling. This letter was in Spanish. I briefly described the encounter and mentioned how I found out about him from Eduardo, his former student. The answer came in twenty two days. Jacob was not the man I saw, but he was so curious about my search, that he offered friendship and possible assistance in my quest.

I felt grateful and a bit disappointed. Obviously, Antwerp had some other offerings for me. Naturally, I planned on visiting the city whenever possible, but at the same time, I hoped for some kind of message that would lead me to my beloved Priest. I kept on asking my Divine Mother.

On the night of twenty first to twenty second of June 1989 I pray Love Rosary as usual. I could feel a gentle freezing sensation coming from my feet toward my face. All of a sudden, a current of wind, like a vortex, takes me out of my body into the unknown space. Instantly, I am placed in a room with bookshelves and desks with chairs. It looked like a library. There I see my beloved Priest standing, conversing with some other man of his height. They both notice me and stop talking, looking at me. Rapidly floating toward my beloved I reach with my right hand to touch his left arm. I feel the flesh - it was warm. He wore a safari type outfit, with short sleeve shirt and slacks. My touch caused me to return quickly in the same vortex and I find myself floating, being surrounded by many masks of light electric blue colour, introducing themselves to me one by one. After maybe ten of them I find myself in my body again, trying to feel the toes first. It wasn't coming easily.

I am still holding the beads between my fingers. Would repetition and mantra of Love Rosary be this effective? What was the message behind this event? Am I to look for him in the library? This was by far the most intimate contact we've made since our encounter. Interestingly, we were entering the same sign - the Cancer.

How much Destiny was there involved in my experience, or how much Desire had created the result? When we ask, we shall receive and we do receive. Is it right to ask then? How can we possibly have a wisdom of knowing what's the best for us?

I began to include the Lord's Prayer. It is more submissive and I truly wanted that which I deserved and was ready for. There was another gift sent to me. It was again audible and had a very specific instruction about my personal spiritual direction. Neither this one can be shared. It empowered me tremendously and confirmed to me that I was on the right track.

The summer was challenging. Our vegetable garden helped us to survive. We were asked to move out. The eviction notice was written by Verne's lawyer. I asked to stay in the house until it sells, so that in the meanwhile, I might be able to find something affordable. I needed to turn to a subsidized housing, but the waiting list was too long. A small financial settlement I received from Verne could support us for three more months. I was resourceful enough to stretch it upto Christmas. Worrying solves nothing. I had to focus on positive aspects of life to keep my sanity.

When the children start school, I am totally involved with them. Then, there is time for nothing else.

The last week of summer vacation I went to a social gathering where the invited speaker introduces a forthcoming seminar or promotes some kind of teaching. This time the invited speaker talked about Hermetism. Ray came along with me. The night before going to the lecture I felt an inner excitement and in the lecture room it intensified. I look around. Among familiar faces I observe few newcomers, but my eyes were fixed on the germanic face of a young man in his late thirties, who was absorbed in the presentation. When the lecture was over, one of the friends insists I must meet Marc. He introduces me to that young man.

Marc just came from Belgium. I asked him if he was from Antwerp, but he said he was from Gent. We liked each other. He was a distributor of a very unusual product called Vitaflorum. I asked him to come to my place and tell me more about it. He wrote down my phone number.

Ray looked at me from the corner of his eye.

"Ingrid, you might had met your messenger! How is your gut doing now?"

"Ray, do you realize how close Gent is to Antwerp? Marc speaks excellent English. He must have some promising connections! Why would he show up in this lecture? How many people are interested in Hermetism, really?"

I was ecstatic and more so when I thought of Marc.

He came in the afternoon. He and his family moved to Canada just a month ago in hope of a better future for their four children.

Marc came from Gent, but he grew up in Antwerp and lived there upto recent years. He knew many people in that city who were involved in personal and spiritual growth. When I described my beloved Priest, his mind went blank. Later on during a visit he speaks of his teacher, whose name was Josef. He was a priest. His features were similar to my beloved's. Marc's mother was a teacher in the same school. Marc promised that he'll find out more from his mother.

Within a month I had Josef's phone number. Marc warned me that Josef was married and had children. He obviously left Church. It was fine with me.

One late night I gathered some courage and phoned Josef's number. He answered. I asked him if he was in Santiago de Chile on that particular day or knew of someone from his ranks who travels there occasionally. Josef asked me first why I was looking for that person. He already knew that Marc gave me his number. I told him it was personal but that I could explain more in the letter. He gave me his address and insisted that I must write him about it soon and that he'll answer.

When I hung up the phone, I was soaked in my own perspiration. His beautiful tenor voice still resonated in my ears. He must had been a great chanter. I tried to attach Josef's voice to my beloved's body. It fitted perfectly.

I bought some very special writing paper with matching envelopes and scented it with rose fragrance. The whole letter was written in calligraphy and mailed by registered mail.

In the meanwhile, I began to plan a trip to Europe. Logically, it was an impossible dream. I was at the end of my resources, had nothing to sell, no job, except some babysitting to do and, had four children to feed. Neither did I know my future address. But, I had faith, I had love, I had hope. I had it all!

I chose to fight the eviction in the court. The Subsidized Housing Cooperative did not have any unit available for us yet. The judge didn't give me any chance to speak for myself. Verne's lawyer was quick to speak and I didn't know when there was a right time to say something. A decision was made: a court order for an eviction for mid of November. I had one week to find a place and had a little money left. I told the judge that he made a decision without hearing my story. He heard me out but stated that a made decision cannot be changed but they'll discuss my case in Chambers. I couldn't believe the injustice and wondered how many poor people go to jail because they have no money for a lawyer. And on top of that, I had to call the judge "Mi Lord"! I broke down. In tears, I went to the office of the housing cooperative. They must had taken pity on me because the receptionist gave me an address of the unit that would be available right after Christmas. I reserved a unit with a small payment.

I phoned Verne's lawyer and told him about my move after Christmas. He said that I cannot go against a court order and that we will be thrown out on the street, regardless of the weather. I didn't believe him. I inquired other places about this law. The lawyer was right. I phoned Verne. I didn't speak with him for several months now. He was reluctant about giving us an extension. He wanted to sell his house quickly. I had to go deeply into his conscience. Then, he agreed. It had to pass another court hearing, but it became legal. Only after moving out I was in title to another small financial settlement that would support us for four more months. Marc helped me in the meanwhile with a small loan.

This winter was too cold. In my heart I had warmth. Letters from Christian and Jacob kept on coming regularly and I answered them within a few days. Whenever I had a spare moment, I taped some Christmas music with a few carols I sang myself. These were Christmas gifts for friends I loved. Twice a week I went for rehearsals for our upcoming concerts.

In December I was astonished by the news: General Pinochet stepped down to give way to a more democratic leadership in Chile and around that time the Berlin wall was taken down. Synchronicity? That would be impossible to sell to me. Someone is playing the Almighty. I chose to skip the three capital letters that came to my mind. Obviously, the events are predestined. I stopped trusting history again. Some say that history is written in the stones of the Great Pyramid. Nostradamus prophesied many events but at the end of his life he stated that we have the power to change the future. I believed in that power.

I decided to remain positive and give power to the forces of Light that will lead humanity into Freedom. I made a promise to myself that the following summer I will visit Europe and my country. When I left Bohemia, I never hoped to be able to return. The military communist system was there to stay for a long time. Now they talked about a democratic election and a candidate who was a prominent prisoner for many years, a writer with suspiciously short pants which had to be noticed by everyone. They must have shrunk during his visit to the United States.

When we are in the middle of chaos, we lose the sight and understanding. We become the confusion itself. Only an outsider can see clearly what's going on. The same thing was happening with my search. At times, when I was so absorbed in my desire to find my beloved soon, I was losing a clarity.

Marc was going to visit his family in Belgium for New Year. He asked me to come along and meet Josef. It was not feasible for me. Marc was going to visit him and perhaps bring me the answer. He helped me yet with moving prior to his leaving.

We had a humble Christmas but were not depending on anyone. I invested a part of my little settlement into a line of product that was very sellable and could support us. I became an enterpreneur of the nineties, not knowing where the next meal was coming from, but positive and doing the best every day.

Anxiously I've been waiting for Marc's call from Belgium. He phoned me after his return. Josef told him that my letter was already answered. Waiting for it every day became exciting - I might receive good news afterall.

A n s w e r e d   P r a y e r

On some days I was getting a response from the potential customers. Some people offered to organize a home show. Sometimes I made some money, but mostly I had to invest them back into buying a new product. Not many multilevel marketing companies allow the freedom. Many put conditions. Mine did. It became a struggle. Despite my faith, I worried. Fortunately, I could sew. I made myself a classy wardrobe from the remnants that cost almost nothing. I had to look presentable. The way to a success is a long way and it takes many hours of work without pay. Some days I felt discouraged. Hours on the phone and hardly any business. I became stressed and could feel it in my body. Fatigue became a burden of my daily life. We couldn't eat properly anymore - most of our diet were potato dishes, legumes and bread that I made.

If I didn't have Hanna to talk to, I would have much tougher time in dealing with crisis. She always said that I was a survivor and make good things happen.

"Ask!" she said. "Why don't you ask for more business?".

She felt I was not aggressive enough in my prayers. That was a new attitude for me. The truth is that I never knew how to ask for myself. I did it for everyone else but myself. Why not try? My friends Jacob and Christian were praying for me, as they claimed. Why couldn't I? I wrote down what I needed: just enough money to get to Europe and back and for my current expenses for my family while I am gone. My prayer was spoken and visualized in detail. After the ritual, I slept very peacefully. I decided not to worry anymore and to surrender completely.

The following week became very busy. I had a show with good sales almost every night and more shows were booked. The airline was paid for the ticket. Other shows provided funds for other expenses.

Before the end of May I was flying home to Europe. I didn't have to worry about the lodging either. Jacob had a place for me in Antwerp and the rest would be provided by the Universe. Once I get home to Bohemia, I can stay with some of my friends and relatives who will hopefully recognize and remember me. I had no time to notify anyone except Jacob by phone. So far, I had no answer from Josef. I assumed that the letter got lost. The same phenomenon happened a few years ago with letters to Rosa's family. None arrived. Obviously, I was supposed to go personally and check things out on my own.

Just a couple of days prior to my departure to Europe, a friend, who was at some kind of conference in Montreal, brought me a cassette tape to listen to. It was entitled "The Future Self". It explains the nineties and late eighties in terms of changes that are due to cosmic energy causing our glandular system to respond. In some bodies the changes will be less favourable, in others very positive. It all depends on the attitude of the mind and the body's readiness to changes. Diet and cleansing was highly stressed. Intuition would be the language of the future. The woman speaker talked about an incredible acceleration of events and of the coming together of science, art, and philosophy. Based on our commitment in daily practice, we can actively participate in the outcomes. Every change can be manifested on our plane of existence when our minds allow it to actualize itself. Our mind is the doorway and we have that power to make things happen. In other words, the Creator is powerless without our permission to act. She also spoke about December 14th, 1989. Due to an astrological event and some retrogates, the old dictatorship systems had to give way to a new order of mankind's unity.

Wow! It was powerful! I was ecstatic about this information and felt absolutely comfortable about my specific requests in my prayers. Again, I was reminded how important each of us is in the vast Universe. This realization was my armour for the trip. I just knew that this trip will make a difference in mine and other people's lives.

Ingrid Heller

Antwerpen

Directly from Amsterdam I went by train to Antwerp, enjoying the site of typical Dutch apartments with windows dressed in white lacy curtains. Toward the Belgian border the style has changed. There is a marked difference between the styles of the two countries.

Travelling by train is very much like travelling in life. Places and people come your way when you are there in its own time and space. All you have to do is to be there and observe what's going on. It is much better to be awake or, the opportunity to experience something particular will never come back again. At the crossroads there is more activity. Direction signs, people waiting or running, some loaded with heavy luggage, some travel lightly.

Again, I was reminded of the illusion of being in motion when the train on the parallel rail starts to move and you actually believe that yours is moving. There is always a feeling of fear associated with it. Fear of leaving too soon, not being ready for a departure, or leaving without the party you're travelling with. I remembered this fear from my childhood, when I was travelling by train with my mother. It happened at the crossroads with a longer stop, when she went to get me a lemonade, leaving me by the window so I could see her. Another train came by and I lost the sight of her. I was afraid that she would board the other train instead. Then the train moved and I feared that my mother was left behind. Only after a while, when the other train was gone, I realized that we were still waiting, I felt safe again. At the crossroads it is better to look ahead.

Before I realized, two hours passed and the train was arriving to Antwerpen Centraal. I was instructed to get off at Berchem, the next stop. Jacob was either to meet me there, or, I was to phone him. I had to phone. He gave me an address to get to by taxi. It was just three blocks away. It was the home of his parents. They were the sweetest old people I've met in a long time. Jacob was on his way.

Even though I had a photograph of Jacob, I couldn't imagine him the way he is. He came with a sincere smile and lit up face He gave me a brotherly kiss and bubbled words of welcome both in Spanish and French, so his parents could participate. Obviously, they must had known something about me from Jacob.

That same afternoon he took me to Deurne and showed me a parish to which I sent my card. Now Jacob worked as a chaplain in the institute for handicapped in Brecht, where he was much happier. He liked to work with children.

Later, he drove me to a park that was very special to him. It is called Boeckenberg, meaning the 'Book mountain'. It was his favourite place ever since his childhood. He learned how to swim in the local swimming pool.

We walked on the path slowly, getting used to each other's accents. The aged tall trees witnessed the conversation of the two people who had a lot in common.

70

The Divine Comedy II by Beatrice

We both loved children, were devotional in a healthy way, loved outdoors and classical music.

He asked me what my plans were and I told him that I thought of visiting Lourdes and going home to Bohemia for three weeks. He was happy to hear about Lourdes.

"Sister, you wrote me once that you would like to be baptized by immersion and asked me if I could baptize you. You don't need me for that. I am just a simple priest. In Lourdes you can be baptized in holy water. Nobody will ask you any questions. Baptism is for everyone, just like the Sun is for everyone. Nobody asked me any questions there. When I was immersed I felt like a milllion dollar man and could hardly feel the cold water. You're going to Lourdes for your baptism, Ingrid!"

"Actually, Jacob, I am going there for other reasons. I must see the church's interior and I will probably meet someone interesting there."

"Do not tell me, sister, that you hope to find your man there! He is not a priest. The man you are looking for is more special. Seek and you shall find!"

We came to a bridge that connected the both banks of a large man made pond. Jacob became silent for a while. He points at the cress molded into a stone railing and shows me the Latin words engraved in it.

"This message is for you, Ingrid: NEC FALLERE, NEC FALLI."

Silence continues the message. I felt the meaning but lacked the ability to express it verbally.

"What does it mean, Jacob?"

"DO NOT DECEIVE, DO NOT BE DECEIVED..., Ingrid, you are looking for love believing that the man you saw on the street of Santiago can return your love to you.What if he cannot? There may be another reason for your quest, Ingrid! Remember, our heart is not quiet until it finds what it is looking for. You are not looking for that man. You are looking for love because you already know of such love. Ingrid, there are other men who can offer you that love. Why don't you settle with someone nice, create a family again. Why do you believe that the man you're looking for is the only one who deserves you?"

"I promised him that I'll find him! He wants me to!"

"How can anyone ask of you so much. You travel half the Earth, spend money you don't have, make sacrifices."

"Jacob, I love him! I cannot be involved with anyone else. It is not possible for me. Even if I tried I can't!"

"Well, sister, you must know something I don't know. I became a priest while very young. I never loved a woman."

"Do you regret it?"

"No, I do not. My mission is in my work. Besides, if I were married, who would take you places in Antwerp and take you for a Belgian beer? Come, sister, over there is a nice quiet restaurant. We can have something to eat and toast with beer. I thirst! I thirst for truth, knowledge, and beer. But, before we leave this bridge, I want to show you a secret door."

Jacob leads me to an old wooden door of some shelter or underground storage. "Here the most important writings were stored during the war. There is always a patron who looks after our knowledge."

"Who were the patrons here, Jacob?"

"The Counts of Boeckenberg."

"Was that their cress?"

"Yes, it is their cress, Ingrid. Now, come, I am thirsty!"

Jacob offers me his arm and leads me toward the restaurant in the middle of the woods. We were the only guests. In our conversation we talked about my children, Eduardo and Jacob's years in Chile. We planned for the following day after he'd serve the morning mass in the Institute's church. Jacob was going to show me real Antwerpen, with Rubens' works, statue of ogre and the largest gothic cathedral of Belgium, dedicated to Our Lady. I enjoyed every moment with Jacob, who physically was an attractive Flemish type, but looked nothing like my beloved.

When we returned to his parents' home, he showed me a room I could use. It used to be his bedroom but for many years now he resided in places of his work. After a long trip and a busy day I slept extremely well..

A l c h e m i s t

The early morning airplanes woke me up, but I already had my seven hours of sleep. Later on I found out from Jacob's mother that we were near the Deurne International Airport. I had time to myself. I was anxiously waiting for a later hour to phone Josef. In the meantime, I wrote in my Journal about all that had transpired. I described Jacob in one long paragraph. He had the title of a "Brother" who was known by me before we had met. I forgot to ask him about the meaning of his name. Jacob is James, the Spanish call James either Jaime or Santiago. I made a connection to Jacob through Santiago. His surname is De Schryver. What does that mean? I contemplated all the messages I received in the outer world: Boeckenberg, the secret door to knowledge, the cress with a LION and the powerful words.

Toward eight o'clock I dialed Josef's number. A woman's voice told me that he only comes for weekends. He was working in Holland. I had only three days to wait.

After a lovely continental breakfast and Mme De Schryver's constant talking, Jacob came over to pick me up. I appreciated the French spoken in their family. Madame was my number one teacher. She introduced me to television news, excited about an upcoming democratic election in Czechoslovakia. She thought it was unusual to have a writer for a candidate. Then she said that their family name means THE WRITER.

Tramway number thirteen took us to the Green Square with the famous statue of Peter Paul Rubens and an overpowering nearby tower of the Cathedral of Our Lady.The charming cobble stone street lined with outdoor coffee shops guided us to the main door of the cathedral.

Having a passion for forms I spent most of the time in front of huge Flemish paintings and statues of Peter and Paul which were by the main corridor. Peter held two keys in his hand. I pointed it out to Jacob and asked him if he knew why he had two keys to Heaven. Jacob had his answer immediately:

"One key is made of gold. It opens the door of male energy. The other key is made of silver that opens the door of female energy. Like Sun and Moon."

"Where did you get this explanation, Jacob? Catholics didn't teach you this! Do you actually know what you're talking about?"

"I figured that wisdom is hard to obtain, so I read. I read it somewhere."

In a soft voice to preserve a quiet atmosphere, I collaborated: "Sun and Moon are used in Alchemy as symbols of balance between male and female energy. Lunar way is the inner way to enlightenment. Solar way is the external way. Both should be balanced and reflecting each other, just like the moonlight reflects the sunlight. Some say that Peter represented the inner sexuality which ultimately leads to spirituality. Peter also represented the corner stone of the Church. Therefore, the key is the balance of female and male energies within us to open the door to Kingdom of Heaven."

Jacob had no comment. I probably shouldn't mention sexuality. People have a hang up over the word, thinking only in terms of genitality and intercourse. We proceeded further into the cathedral. Jacob took some time for himself, kneeling in front of a sculpture of Mary with the child. They both had Royal robes and a Crown. By its side I saw incredible wood carvings of apostles. My attention was focused on St. John, holding a Chalice. His face was refined and very feminine. The artwork in the cathedral was truly a treasure. I decided to come back. We had many other places to see.

From the Steen that was guarded by an ogre at the entrance overseeing the nearby port on Schelde river, we went back toward the cathedral, passing by the City Hall and another sculpted formation dealing with the conflict between humans and giants. Soon we were on another street full of shops. Jacob stopped by one of them:

"Ingrid, I come here to buy books once in a while. Come with me, you will like it."

I look up above the door to read the sign. It reads DEN ALCHEMIST. The Alchemist.

I was inside the store instantly. As soon as the lady clerk was free, I faced her with a question: "I was supposed to meet someone here. He is a very spiritual man, tall, handsome, in his forties."

She passed me a business card saying, "Then you should talk to Mr. Jan Snijder. He is such a man."

I read the card. Jan is an astrologer, psychologist. He lives on Golden Flee Street! I immediately thought of the story about Argonauts and Jason. The lady clerk observed me. I turn to her with another question:

"What street are we on? What is your address?"

"We are on STEENHOUWERSVEST, the Free Masons Street. But it relates to the ones who had a breast plate."

She smiles very kindly at me. A sisterly soul!

Buzzing was the right word for my feelings. I was on the right track! Jacob observed us and perceived that something good was happening. I told the lady that I'll be back yet. She was easy to talk to. Her English was impecable.

Jacob looked over my shoulder to read the card:

"Guldenvliestraat... that's in Berchem! The tram goes by. It is one street from Osylei, just three blocks from my parents' house. Do you want to take a tram there?"

"It would be faster, wouldn't it? Let's go, Jacob, something is beginning to happen in Antwerpen after all!"

Like two happy kids we strode quickly back to Green Square to get on our tramway. The number thirteen was just arriving. Europe is so condensed. When you take public transportation and get to your destination in no time, you wonder why you didn't walk. From the tram stop we crossed one corner and appeared on a steep narrow sidewalk of Guldenvliestraat. We checked the numbers. Indeed, Jan's name was on the door bell. Jacob prevented me from ringing it:

"Sister, they must be having lunch now. My mother has a lunch ready for us. Let us go there first and then you can visit with Jan. You know your way now."

I agreed. Two hours later I was back in the same location. I pressed the doorbell. The door was opened by a tall handsome man with dark hair and blue eyes. I was speechless for a moment. He was the man from my dream who passed me the envelope with a note and an alchemical substance.

"Je voudrais parler avec vous, Monsieur. Est-ce que vous avez un moment?"

He keeps on looking at me with softness and total acceptance of a surprising visit. "Oui, mais je ne parle pas Français.," he apologizes.

"Et moi, je ne parle pas Flamand! Quelle langue parlez-vous?

"English!"

"Me too! Oh, what a relief!" I said while exhaling. I must had held my breath again. "My name is Ingrid Heller. I come from Canada. I must speak with you..."

He invited me in and asked me to wait a moment so he could finish his lunch in a hurry. He opened a door into a room with a chair to sit on and with some antique furniture. With the exception of wall hangings, it looked like a mirror image of the room in the dream I had. The street and the houses of the dream looked almost identical.

I observed a poster of the chart of The Cabbalistic Tree of Life, the map to inner Journey and understanding of life cycles. Three minutes later, Jan opened the glass door to his office and asked me to have a seat by his desk next to him.

"What can I do for you, Ingrid?"

"I was instructed to come to Antwerp. I am looking for a man...."

"That should be easy to find. I suppose you are looking for a special man."

"Exactly! He is in his forties, is tall, handsome, noble looking and is very spiritual. He also writes. I believe I am to find him in this city."

Jan is looking at a fixed point, rubbing his chin, thinking.

"Why Antwerpen?"

"He is either here or someone from Antwerp is to show me the way to him."

"It could be me whom you are looking for. I am forty-two!"

"I already met him. I know what he looks like."

"If you had met him, why do you look for him here?"

"We just saw each other in a real geographical place. We were both visitors there. We also parted from each other without any introduction."

"A typical meeting of the twins. They meet at the crossroads and inspire the highest in each other. You are doing the right thing. Keep on asking at the gates!"

"The Song of Solomon...,. that is what's going on! Do you happen to know anyone of those special qualities here by the name of Josef?"

"In Holland, yes, but not here. I think you should be looking in Holland. There are some like that..."

He paused for a moment. I thought he searched in his memory banks for my man, so, I kept quiet.

"You know, Ingrid, you are very lucky to be at that point of uniting with your beloved. We truly earn it. The Divine Romance is for Divine Lovers. Your name was well chosen for you too: INGRID... you have INRI within your name. Igni Naturae Renovatus Integra. By fire all nature is renewed. Fire of Spirit and Love is that powerful."

The door bell rang. Jan rose from his chair.

"My client is here. Is there a phone number where I could reach you? If something comes my way, I will phone you", he said leading me to the door.

I phoned him and gave him a contact number in Antwerp from Jacob's home. Jan, again, encouraged me not to give up and keep on searching.

The rest of the afternoon Jacob and I passed in the Middelheim park, an outdoor museum with the most interesting sculptures. Some were fascinating. We took several pictures. One of them with a setting of a nobleman at his desk on which there was a book and menora. I sat on his lap. Jacob teased me that I found my man. We called my new immortal friend a DUKE. He had that appearance.

The outdoor restaurant at the park saved the thirsty Jacob again and I gladly joined him in a ritual of appreciating the Belgian beer.Wherever we went, there were all kinds of birds and, Jacob explained that Belgium is rich in fauna. I asked him about herons. He said that by the Dutch border in Berendrecht there is the largest heron colony in Western Europe. He offered to take me to Reigersbos in two days.

.   The next day I had to myself. Jacob had to work. I went again to Den Alchemist with the intention of collecting more information. I noticed that they had a place for flyers. Two of them were appealing and I decided to follow up on them.

On the way back I visited the cathedral again. Next to the main corridor was a chapel where people found some privacy for prayers. When everyone left, I went to read from the open Bible on the stand by the altar. The red ribbon bookmark kept the book on the same page. Interestingly, it was dedicated to Mary Magdalene and her virginity. Just like most of churches of Our Lady in France are dedicated to Mary Magdalene, so was this one. It goes together with French speaking nations. This Bible was in French. The royal robe and the crown therefore belongs to Mary Magdalene. Dukes of Brabant used to be rulers of what we presently call Belgium. They must had sponsored construction of many temples.

I walked back to Berchem and enjoyed the atmosphere of this charming old city. Many corner houses had sculptures of the same image of Mary and the child. It probably reflected the wealth of the landlord.

I phoned one number from the flyer. This group made street presentations, acting a play that was intended to attract people interested in the spiritual growth. In Europe everything is hidden, secretive, hermetically sealed. It must be in European genes since the time of inquisition.

I was invited to meet the group. I went the same afternoon. They were lively, friendly, and happy people. I described my beloved and asked whether there is someone like him in Antwerp. They sent me to Nico Thelman's house.

On the way there I stopped by the Rubens House. Another treasure. I loved the garden with statues of Minerva and Mercury and its park-like landscape. Rubens, I hear, was a brilliant man. While painting he had either an intellectual or philosophical discussion and at the same time was dictating a letter to someone. He lived in Love.

Nico received me. He was tall, handsome, and had Flemish features in him. He carried himself with grace. He introduced me to Key Monebo, who is known for tours called "Esoteric Antwerp". It is presently sponsored by the municipality and she added other tours, taking people to museums, churches, streets. Antwerp is full of symbols. It is like a book to read, if one knows how to read it.

Nico felt I should get in touch with Jan Snijder who knows just about anybody on the Path. People come to him for councel, readings, guidance. Nico also felt that I might be able to find that person in Holland. He actually named a library where I could find some answers. He gave me the address and phone numbers, insisting that I must call first to make a reservation. It was a private library.

I became very curious about the founder. His name was Mr. Ritman. He spent his company's profits on purchasing precious manuscripts, had them transcribed and translated into major languages, then published the limited editions of all of them. I was in awe and blessed Mr. Ritman's work.

Nico was an interesting man. On his white half circle shaped desk there was a sculpture of Merlin with a crystal ball in his hand. On the wall he had a poster saying I BELIEVE IN MAGIC. He was a magician of the 21st century and an illusionist. Since his childhood he was offered life experiences which led him to think about nature's laws, about consciousness and the sacred psychology. He said that Jan Snijder understands these laws as well and that he was a true psychologist, just like Carl Jung was.

I wished I could stay at Nico's place longer, but I had to return to De Schryver's home on time, as I promised. Nico insisted I must keep in touch and definitely, must visit Ritman's Library.

In the late evening, after a beautiful supper and conversation with Jacob's parents, I retired. I added another day to my Journal. The day was magical. Nico's name was recorded as The El Man.

The statue
ot St. Peter by Hans van Mildert in the Antwerp's Cathedral of Our Lady.

In Middelheim park in Antwerp on June 1st. 1990 - International Children's Day.

Ingrid Heller

At Reigersbos in Berendrecht.

At Nico's office.

H e r o n

It took less than one hour to get to Berendrecht by car. It was a small organized town. Jacob parked his car by the gateway of Reigersbos, the heron sanctuary. On our right was a restaurant. We walked into a park. It was very natural. It almost looked unkept. After a short walk, a very special house appears in front of us that must had belonged to someone of noble background. On the lawn in front of it we saw few ducks. We continued on the path, avoiding humid areas.

Jacob chatted with a landscaper for a while, who cut the tall grass. They spoke in Flemish. Some words I picked up - many came from German and with little imagination I understood the rest of it. They talked about the man who lived in that white mansion. I could hardly imagine why anyone of good blood would want to live in this wild and humid environment, unless, they had a good reason. The vision of my experience with the heron in a Low Countries' city kept on coming back. In it my beloved had the form of a bird. I had to ask.

"Jacob, who lives in that white mansion?"

"A very well known gentleman. He is the president of the International Olympic Games Committee. He speaks several languages. He is a Count."

"Is he tall, attractive?" I asked anxiously.

"No, he is short."

I thought that Jacob was teasing me again. "Oh, sure. He is short! How do you know, Jacob?"

"I've met him, Ingrid. He is short and older than the man you're looking for."

I was a bit disappointed. Why? If I had no expectations, I would be totally content and glad to be able to see rare birds in their natural habitat, watch their flight from one tree to the other checking on the nests and feeding their young.

Jacob kept on observing me, smiling:. "Ingrid, you are just at the beginning of your quest. Relax, take it easy, enjoy. When you least expect it, what you're looking for will happen. Let go of expectations!"

Jacob was right. Aaron said the same thing to me. "Let go, set the man free."

I had to pose by the sign of the park for another shot of Jacob's camera.

I knew exactly what the next step was: the restaurant. Jacob had a blessed appetite, for his mother was an excellent cook. She was an alchemist in the kitchen. All of the food she prepared was permeated by her love.

We sat by the window and ordered our meal. I needed to get my mind off previous emotions. Luckily, Jacob asked me how my day was yesterday. This way I had the opportunity to talk about the chapter in the Bible inside the Cathedral.

"Did you know, Jacob, that the Cathedral in Antwerpen is dedicated to Mary Magdalene? Not at all to Jesus' Mother!"

"Where did you get that idea, Ingrid?"

"It is indicated in the Bible there. The page was open where Mary Magdalene is honoured as a Holy Virgin."

"You must had misunderstood! Magdalene was not a virgin, on the contrary!" Jacob became very serious.

"It doesn't speak of physical virginity. It speaks of a pure consciousness that was immaculate. Do you understand, Jacob?"

"You have lost me here. Are you speaking of immaculate conception?"

"Yes, I am! She must had been pure! Why would Jesus love her and allow her to cleanse his feet? Jacob, I think that immaculate conception is taking place in consciousness. The birth of Christ! The birth of Virgin of the World!"

I had nothing more to say on the subject. Jacob was thinking about what I said. I introduced him to something that has threatened his programming. I chose not to continue the subject. I appreciated him as he was. I told him that I had met some interesting people and the guide of "Esoteric Antwerp". He was pleased that I managed to visit Ruben's House.

Our lovely lunch was sealed in our stomachs by the most delicious Belgian chocolates. The master chocolate maker lives in Antwerp.

In the afternoon Jacob took me to the Institute by Brecht where he worked. The park on the property was absolutely beautiful. Mature trees of many kinds, blooming rhododendrons, pathways filled with yellow sand. The architecture of the Institute was quite modern. Everything was well planned, with classrooms, gym, pool, dining rooms, and plenty of light coming through many windows.

Jacob showed me the inside of the joined church. It was spacious and magnificent looking. There was an emblem above the altar. I had difficulty seeing at the distance. I asked Jacob what it was.

"It is a symbol of Christ feeding his young by the sacrificial blood of his heart. This symbol can be found in Europe in some places that were founded by altruistic families."

"This is the bird that came to me, Jacob!. Is he a heron?"

"No, sister. He is a pelican, the fisher bird."

I had to sit down for a while. Dizziness came over me. The understanding of my experience was coming to me. I was kissed by a pelican. Who is my beloved? Did I have to come to Antwerp to understand the symbol? Yet, this was just a part of the symbol, just the beginning. Jacob sat down next to me. He offered to be my confessor.

"Jacob, there is nothing to confess. There is something to share. This bird has guided me to Europe and to Antwerp."

"Then you are in the right place. I should show you another building with this emblem. It is on the mansion of the counts of Boeckenberg."

"Where is their mansion, Jacob?"

"In Boeckenberg park. I am surprised I didn't show it to you. I wanted to."

"You thought of beer! That is why you want to go there again," I teased him.

"It will be a pleasant addition to it. Ingrid, I know you like symbols. I will show you a small sculpture of Saint Michael in the church of Brecht.

Before we left, Jacob invited me to his residence for a cup of tea. He had to check his phone messages. To my pleasant surprise he had three flags on his bureau: Belgian, Canadian, and a Chilean. The rotating globe next to them was positioned on both Americas. Then Jacob showed me a box where he kept all my letters. He had them numbered. It was sweet. He was not a lonely person, but he learned to like me and appreciate me. Doubtlessly, we were friends crossing each other's paths.

Saint Michael's statue was just a little over one foot tall. Michael had his arm positioned as if he held a spear. The sculptor never gave him one.

"What do you think, Ingrid? Any ideas?"

"It reminds me of the wood carving by Rudolf Steiner. It is in Goetheannum. He called it a "Representative of Man". A weary looking man with condemned beings in hell under his feet and next to him an angelic winged being. He is in the middle of it, holding his left arm in the same position, having no weapon. I would call it a "Spiritual Warrior". Weapon is the mind and the heart, love the Truth enough so that we'd defend it with our mind in the action of speaking, writing, and thinking."

"You make a very good student, Ingrid. Actually, you are a teacher."

Then Jacob showed me an icon painting where baby Jesus looks very frightened and loses his little shoe. Jacob had an explanation: "Jesus had a vision of his crucifixion that had scared him. He trembled so much that he lost his little shoe."

I really liked this idea.

In the evening back in Antwerp I phoned Josef's house. There was no answer. Neither in the morning. I felt a bit restless and decided to leave for my trip to Lourdes. Jacob took me to the train station to make sure that I leave on the right train to Paris. I had to change in Brussels anyway. I left some of my luggage with his parents and brought what I needed for Czechoslovakia. I was coming back before my final departure from Amsterdam. I wanted to spend a few more days in Antwerp and around Jacob's family. I loved their presence.

Home Boeckenberg in Deurne, with the Pelican symbol.

In Louvre museum in Paris with God Mercury.

From Louvre to Lourdes

From the Northern Train Station in Paris I took a taxi to my friends' place They had a bed for me. After two nights and one day in Paris I was going to take a train to Lourdes.

My friends had a ticket to Louvre for me and drove me there the next morning. Entering through a pyramid into the museum is like entering through a dimension of time into timeless space where present, past, and future coexist at any given moment. I had seen so many treasures of art in my life, but was always eager to place more of them into my mind's memory. I took almost a whole day in the museum, enjoying the exposition and the rooms themselves. Incredible scenes were painted onto walls and ceilings, just to compliment the beauty of it all.

After many hours in the museum I walked through the streets of central Paris. This city is very well planned and at any season is beautiful. Before coming to Canada, I spent two months in Paris. The city was well known to me.

At the end of the day I went to purchase a train ticket for Lourdes. I could only afford a one way ticket. It was costly and I didn't have enough money for a return. I decided to trust the Universe and take chances. I had to be in Lourdes.

It was an eight hour ride. The sky was cloudy, it was about to rain.

I just made it inside the cathedral of Lourdes and, it began to pour. They were about to commence with the mass. This one was in French. I observe the interior, ceilings, and altar. Everything was the way I saw it in my Mother's Day experience in 1980! My beloved was behind the altar at that time. Will I find him here again?

I took a seat in one of the benches and gave thanks for being there. The church was filling up quickly. Everyone wanted to be sheltered.

During the mass I perceived a nice energy right behind me. From the singing I knew he was a man. He had a clear pitch baritone voice and had no problems with French. When we were lining up for the Eucarist, he waited for me, reserving a space in front of him for me. Was he ever charming! About forty seven, tanned complexion, quite tall. I couldn't place him into any ethnic group. Toward the end of the mass we wished each other a peace. I wished him in English, so he did to me. When the mass was over, I turned toward him with a common statement: "You look very familiar to me. Have we met before?"

"I am not sure. Are you here with a group?"

"No, I am by myself." I expected our conversation to continue, instead, he looked at the black and white tile floor and proceeded slowly toward the door. It was a very unusual reaction to what I said. I gathered he was in some kind of commitment and chose not to talk to any woman. After I inspected the church, I went outside toward grotto and piscines. The rain subsided. I covered my hair with a long white scarf and wrapped it around my neck. My whole body was protected by a llama poncho I had brought from Chile. By the grotto many faithful and sick were praying. People were filling up bottles with holy water or drinking it directly. I tried some too. It was cold but created a heat in my stomach.

I went to buy spring water in the store so I could use the bottle for a refill. With my last few franks I bought a barguette that would last me upto Czechoslovakia. I had only a few coins left. I could afford going to a public bathroom only twice. Eating little helped. Around the Lourdes cathedral you can hear coming from sound system speakers announcements in many languages. They announced the Rosary procession by the grotto for the evening. Thousands began to gather shortly after. I was getting cold so I went to warm up from the candles lit up by worshippers. There were hundreds of them. The place was by the piscines and provided a partial roof.

Someone sitting on a bench near the grotto shifted to give me a seat. I took my Rosary and participated in prayers and singing. I could see everyone in the procession as they were passing by.

The Irish chantress had a gorgeous voice. She sang a large repertoire of Ave Marias. People were asked to say prayers into a microphone in their language. There was a male voice speaking Czech. And more Ave Marias. .

For a while I closed my eyes, trying to feel the crowd and the truth. When I opened my eyes, I saw that nice man in the procession, holding a Rosary and very devotionally praying. I observed his every move, his strong hands gliding on the stone in the grotto, his slow graceful gait, his well formed body. He was rare. Not many of his kind survived the modern times. Then he disappeared in the crowd. There was no way I could locate him again. It was dark and, people covered the grounds everywhere. He was a mystery person, who behaved in a different way. During my Santiago encounter I behaved in a different way and regretted it since then.

After I took my turn in the procession, it was almost over. Not knowing where I'll stay for the night, I checked the grounds. Roofed wheel chairs were everywhere. There was one under a large tree near the bathrooms that would provide protection for the night. It began to rain again. I went to warm up from the candles again, but people blocked the access. When I approached the place from the other side, I was drawn toward a particular spot. No one was standing there. I stretched my hands toward the heat and light and saw another pair of hands lighting a candle. I look up and see that nice man.

He is watching me in disbelief. "My first wish came true!" he said to me. "I wrapped a paper full of wishes around the candle. To see you again was the first one on my list."

"What was the second one?" I asked.

"To follow my heart and never give to structured planning again. All my life I've been following the voice of my heart and now my psychologist tells me that at the age of forty six I must make a goal and plan for it. She thought I was immature. Today was my first day of planning. I bought a train ticket to Holland and made reservations for supper in a restaurant. Then I met you at the mass and wanted to speak with you, but couldn't because of my previous commitment to myself. I didn't enjoy one single bite. I thought of you and how wonderful it would be to share my meal with you, have you by my side in the procession, pray with you and hold your hand.... My train is leaving in one hour...."

We both felt a sadness of parting, yet, we've just met.

"I'll walk you to the station. We have one hour." I answered and walked over to his side of the candle tray and introduced myself:: "My name is Ingrid. I also hoped to see you."

"I am Frank. I spent two weeks here in silence. I had to go through this process. You were the first person I talked to. I knew I'd meet you here. I just knew that someone like you was coming. I was in prayer and meditation a lot. You were on your way."

"I arrived this afternoon and am leaving tomorrow. I had to see this place and wanted to be immersed in holy water."

Frank was very happy about my decision "Ingrid, it is like a baptism. I went through it twice."

I had to laugh. "Frank, as a good catholic you should believe in one baptism only."

"I do, Ingrid. I wanted to be cleansed in my spirit. You understand, don't you?"

"Of course, I do. Who taught you to pray Rosary so well?"

"My mother did. It is her Rosary. When she was dying, she asked everyone of her eight children what they wanted. I asked for her Rosary beads."

I was touched by this story. He was truthful.

We walked up the hill, toward the train station. We talked about our trip over here and who we were in real life. I told Frank the truth about myself, but didn't mention that I was looking for my beloved. He might had misunderstood. I told him that I was on my pilgrimage.

Frank was an engineer and worked in many countries. Like every other good Dutchman he spoke five languages. Presently, he was in the process of a change into a more structured and settled life. He lived with a psychologist who was trying to help him with that. He wasn't sure that her ideas were for him.

"My life was rich in experiences. When I followed my heart, I was happy. Now, I am planning. There is no excitement in it and I realized today that it cannot work for me."

"Life meets us, Frank. We don't meet Life. It can actually be harmful to your personal development to set a program, schedule tomorrows. Life goes from one point to the other."

Frank was concerned about me staying by myself overnight without any reservations for lodging. He wished he could miss the train, but his friend psychologist was waiting for him on arrivals in Holland. He was split. His heart wanted him to stay, duty called for commitment.

It still rained but we didn't feel it. Continuing on our way to the train station, we kept on immersing in each other's energy, without any physical contact.

"You feel like a dear soul to me, Ingrid. For how many past lives have we known each other?"

The street lights revealed the reflection of tears in his eyes. I was unable to hide mine. We had a minute on the platform. The sound of the train brakes cut into our last words of parting. We had each other's address and a hope to keep in touch.

I saw him waving while the train went into motion. I watched until the last wagon disappeared on the horizon. Terrible sadness came over me. He was gone.

I walked back slowly. Some pedestrians crossed the street to the other side to avoid me. I guess they didn't trust my poncho. I probably looked like a gypsy. My blond hair was covered, my face hidden under a hood.

There were some people praying for healing by the grotto. I noticed that most of the crutches hanging there were very old. Selfhealing is a long process. Frank was trying to heal himself but was already realizing that going against himself will take him nowhere. I went to check on his candle. The flame died. I lit it up again and I watched over it until all of the paper spiraling around it was burnt. I wanted his wishes to come true.

The security guards found me in the cart and offered me the use of a mattress by the piscines. They regretted they didn't see me earlier. There was more room in the Inn for pilgrims. I was privileged to have a personal body guard. I fully trusted this one.

The area was very quiet for fourteen minutes. Every fifteenth minute was filled with loud Ave Maria played by the basilica's clock chimes. I had a hope to sleep for a few hours. I dreamt about people, lots of people. They were unknown to me, yet, very familiar. I spoke in many languages to them and I spoke them very well.

In the morning I warmed up with a drink of holy water and went for the first mass. This one was in Italian. I sat at the far corner of the right wing and slept through most of the service. The janitor let me rest until the second mass.

Anxiously I waited by the gate of the piscines for my baptism. A very kind man had me to sit on a chair by the door just for a moment until I was welcomed by a nun in a nurse's uniform. She took me to the ladies' section and had me to wait two minutes, during which I had a chance to read instructions. A curtain opened and I was invited in. There were three other women of all ages and shapes getting dressed. I was offered a cape to place over my nude body. With gentle care the nurses helped me undress.They all had consideration for modesty. I waited for my turn. Another curtain opened and the brilliant sunlight coming through the glass roof embraced me. Three nuns were to assist me. One asked what language I spoke and I said that French was fine. She asked if I preferred English. I agreed to English. She asked me to make a promise to Mary and step into a pool to kiss her statue. At that point my cape was removed from me and two nuns were leading me into a cold water pool made of stone, praying for me. After the kiss the nuns immersed me in the water and offered their hands to lead me out. I was extremely joyous. This was the baptism I wanted! I kept on thanking them. Wearing my cape again, I entered the change room, where equal attention was given to me.

When I stepped outside, I felt renewed. It wasn't a self suggestion. I felt fantastic! I had no other motivation to stay in Lourdes any longer. I walked in the direction of the highway to hitchhike to Bordeaux and then to Paris. It was a long trip and I needed more than luck to get to Paris on the same day.

The first passing car stopped. The driver said he was going to Peau. I joined him but five minutes later I realized that he was lying to me. Fortunately, he let me go. I walked a few meters along the highway when a red sports car squeeked its brakes. He was going to Bordeaux. The Portuguese driver must had been a car racer. I asked angels for protection. Again, I was glad to survive this ride.

It was raining in Bordeaux. I walked over a one hour to the exit highway.

Again, the first car stopped. The driver was from Lourdes and was going to Tours, which was much closer to Paris. He was a good man, in his fifties. I trusted him. He invited me for a lovely supper in Tours, passed me his hotel room and the next morning picked me up for breakfast and took me to the train station, supplying me with a ticket to Paris. I couldn't believe his generosity. He was a part of the Providence, no doubt.

I still had holy water and bread for my trip back home.

Interior of the Basilica of the Rosary in Lourdes where the Masses were served.

M a g i c   F l u t e

I traveled to Prague by train on the day of democratic election. Václav Havel won, of course. I had a precious time with my friends and relatives, visiting places of my childhood and teens, taking pictures everywhere. In June, theaters are still in season and I had a fortune to get tickets for "La Bohème" and an Opera Debut Matinée.

On both performances I ran into my professor, so he invited me to talk to the students and surprise the other professors. To my surprise, they never forgot the rebel. We had a great time together.

I visited some castles and churches, tasted good Bohemian beer, and enjoyed my stay. The three weeks passed quickly. The visit is worth another novel.

Before my departure for Belgium, I had two days in Prague. My dream came true: I got tickets to the National Theatre. It was through a friend who knew that I was coming and she reserved them for me. I went with my two lady cousins.

Our seats were in the first row, centre, first balcony. Incredible! Opera? Magic Flute! My favourite! My cousins and I loved the evening. The opera was in Czech language, but the original libretto was not respected by the translator. The meanings were lost.

On the way back to Belgium I regressed in my memory to the"Magic Flute" performance I saw in Canada in the spring of 1989:

One evening after our rehearsal of Bach Choir I was dropping off my friend Rick. He was a student of music and was blessed with a clean baritone voice. He invited me to join him for the opera.

"You've been a helpful friend and I know you like Mozart, Ingrid. It would be my honour."

It was an emotional moment for me. In those days Verne was difficult to communicate to and I wouldn't have had money for a ticket. Naturally, when I was ready to leave for the opera, Verne made inapropriate remarks on my evening of fun without him.

At that time "Magic Flute" was the perfect message I needed to hear. The English subtitles provided information I appreciated.

Tamino faught a dragon and won. While resting after the battle, he was found by the ladies who were companions of the Queen of the Night, whose daughter Pamina left home to find Truth with the Mystic Brotherhood. The queen showed Pamina's picture to Tamino, who fell in love with her instantly, and then wanted Tamino to rescue her daughter from the influence of the High Priest. Tamino searched for Pamina, meeting Papageno on the way, who dreamt about a woman 'exactly like himself'. Papageno married Papagena. Tamino was given a Magic Flute to guide him on his quest. He found the Brotherhood and was instructed to keep the vow of silence. Pamina was informed about Tamino being in love with her and searching for her. She began her own search for him. When he, because of silence, could not answer her, she mistrusted his love and wanted to take her life away. Instructed by spirits, she persued Tamino. They found each other and were initiated into a higher level by the High Priest and had to pass the test of Fire and Water. Their love saved their souls and the High Priest gave them the title of the 'noble couple'.

I wondered if there was any coincidence between the name PAMELA and PAMINA. The power of my love for my beloved was stronger than nature's call for union with him. I had to find out who he is and then I'd have peace. My intuition hadn't changed: my beloved was also looking for me, in his own way. He had a name for me. For a while I called him Yariek. I trusted that our paths would cross again.

On my return to Antwerp I was to call Josef's home again and might have had some news from Nico or Jan. There was no way I could go to Ritman's Library this time. I couldn't afford a day in Amsterdam. I planned the trip to Holland for the next year. I've met Frank, everyone's directing me to Holland. There must be some answer for me. Everything has its time and its season. I'll wait

The ticket to Magic Flute in The National Theatre in Prague for June 30th, 1990.

H e r m e s

Jacob was very happy to see me again. I had so much to tell him. The De Schryver family received the card I sent them from Czechoslovakia. I was pretty sure that Frank received his by now, with a Belgian phone number on it. Nobody phoned me yet.

Jacob took me again to Boeckenberg. He was such a good listener. Not once would he be judgemental. He heard about Frank, my friends and relatives from my old country, and about other interesting encounters. We walked on the path or sat down on the bench for a while, then walked again. We must had combed the park at least twice. Each time we crossed the bridge, we both looked at the lion cress with Nec Fallere, Nec Falli. Till we walked across the bridge the second time, I remembered the castle of the Counts of Boeckenberg. I became anxious to see their emblem. We walked to the other side of the park. A large meadow spread before us and there was a three story mansion.

Jacob pointed at the emblem above the entrance. "You see, Ingrid, this family has the same emblem that you saw in the church."

For a moment I analyzed the connection between a pelican, myself, and to me these unknown humanitarian families. Why was I standing on that lawn at that time? Should I have gone to the mansion's entrance and ask? Ask what? The pelican I'd seen must had represented more than my christed beloved.

I must had looked perplexed because Jacob took my arm and tried to lead me away.

"Ingrid, this is the right time to have the beer!"

I laughed. The way Jacob said it was amusing and caring at the same time. I let him be the leader.

Conversations across the table have flavour and depth. Social drinking can be an asset.

Jacob took in the first gulp. With foam on his upper lip, that gave him the appearance of a wise man, he finally came up with a question. "Are you sure that you know what you are looking for?"

"Yes and no. What are you trying to tell me, Jacob?"

"Your beloved might have been used as fish bait..."

"Fish bait? Fish bait for what?"

I saw a lovely omniscient spark in Jacob's eyes. He took another gulp and wiped off the foamy mustache. "To lead you to completion, to make a pilgrim out of you, to be guided by the memory of pure love so you don't have to settle for less."

"I don't want to settle for less, Jacob!"

"You meet Frank, other men are drawn to you, your ex-boyfriends are still in love with you. Don't you see the message?"

"Message for what, Jacob?" I couldn't grasp Jacob's suggestion. At times I contemplated on this subject as well. Why am I meeting all these special people? Are they to be my friends, lovers, husbands, teachers, students? What is happening here?

"You are being tested, Ingrid!"

"Tested on what? Fidelity, loyalty, commitment, or what?" Jacob stirred up a defensive force in me. "Don't you know, Jacob, that I am actively looking for my beloved in all the worlds to find him soon, so I can know where I am with him? He may be looking too, you know! Unless I find him, I cannot commit to anyone. As long as I don't find him, I can have fun, that's all I can have...."

"Why are you searching then? Have fun instead!"

"Fun is not satisfying, I long for deep love."

"Ha, I caught you! Your longing is spiritual in nature. You long for God's love. It is not about romance, it is about Divine Romance. Unless you can drink of that cup, you'll thirst! I know about thirst!"

Jacob finished his beer and ordered another one while I was looking into the settled foam in my mug. The foam took the shape of Americas within the circle.of the mug. I was about to show it to Jacob, but the form changed. I was thinking about Jacob's words. He was leading me into the realization of my own quest of my holy grail.

"You look serious, Ingrid! I hope I didn't spoil your enthusiasm...." He clicked his beer mug against mine. "Hey, join me! I cannot enjoy it by myself. Sharing is important."

I pleased him, having a few gulps. "You said it, Jaocb! Sharing is the key. I want to share my quest, my spirituality and love. I already found my love but must find him again!"

"Why did you leave him on that street, then?"

"For loyalty, duty perhaps. In a way I don't know why I did it."

"So you can seek on your own," says Jacob, and looks directly into my eyes.

"You are probably right, Jacob. All that happened to me since that time seems to have a connection. It is like a chain. In a sense it is magical."

"The magic flute!" Jacob gave me a wide smile.

"Have you seen the opera?" I asked him.

"A long time ago. Beautiful music....a very different fairy tale!" Jacob took another gulp in, waiting for my input. I welcomed the opportunity.

"All fairy tales have a deeper meaning behind them. They resonate with children's inner psychology. Magic Flute is made for adults. It made Schikaneder rich. He got kicked out of Free Masonic Brotherhood for it. Apparently, he was not to reveal some of their mysteries to the public. I believe Mozart was excommunicated too."

"What do you think about the secret societies, Ingrid?"

"I guess at some point of our history they had to keep secretive, but I wonder whether it is necessary now."

"They likely practiced that pearls should not be casted before the swine.", Jacob concludes.

"Frankly, Jacob, who has the wisdom to select the elect? There are many wolves in sheep's clothing. If an individual is ready to understand the mystery, it will somehow be revealed to him. A man made initiation in mystery schools is only symbolic."

"Ingrid, did I ever tell you that I appreciate you?"

"Yes, indirectly. Cheers to our friendship, Jacob!"

I raised my mug and toasted to this very special catholic priest. He was my pal.

The evening with Jacob's parents was very pleasant. My French had improved from my visit to France and by my immersion in Czech. Through experience with languages I learned that each time we use one of them, we simultaneously improve in all of them. It must be like a spiral triggering the points in our memory bank, going broader and deeper. The more languages we learn, the easier it is for us to use them. That evening, Jacob left for Brecht.

I chose to return to Den Alchemist book store on the following day. I walked by Josef's house and noticed a car that was not parked there before. Spontaneously, I walked toward the main door and pressed the doorbell. The door was slightly open. My heartbeat accelerated.

I heard Josef's voice saying aloud, "Come in!"

I entered the hallway and respectfully waited for someone. A man in his late forties, dressed in overalls, with pliers in his hand, walked downstairs. He didn't know who I was.

I introduced myself. Josef reached to shake my hand. He seemed gentle, kind, compassionate. Fortunately, I didn't feel embarrassed. I apologized for my previous behaviour. In some aspects Josef resembled my beloved.

"Have you received my letter?" he asked.

"No, I haven't. If I had, I wouldn't had come. Antwerp holds a special post in my life. I had to come."

"Have you found him?"

"No, not yet. But I am getting answers. I am on the right track. Thank-you for your participation, Josef."

"I wish I could be more helpful. I hope you'll find him soon. You'll come back to Antwerp, won't you?"

"I think so. I want to look in Holland too."

I walked toward the door to leave. Josef reached for my hand and squeezed it very compassionately saying, "I wish you all the best, Ingrid!"

As I stepped over their threshold I realized that he was another person I inspired to the quest of true love, that it was worth the effort to find it.

It began to rain. My coat was unpermeable and I always carried an umbrella with me. I walked by Jan's house and later on by Nico's house. It took me about forty minutes to get to Green Square in my highheel shoes. I mastered walking in them since I was fifteen.

On the way I saw many Jewish children and adults. Antwerp seemed to be full of them. Jacob once explained their plain clothing and appearance to me. Women wore wigs. In their tradition, lust had to be conquered by stripping outer beauty and learning to love the essence of the person only. The women shaved their hair and looked very unattractive. It reminded me of cultures where tongues were cut off for false testimonies or hands chopped off for stealing. The human race has gone a long way.

Den Alchemist was open. I was looking around for some kind of a message. I picked a couple of metaphysical cards of artwork and noticed a quarterly publication of a magazine called Den Alchemist. Among many issues there were some from the year 1988. I only had money for one of them. I chose the October issue.

On the way back I stopped by Nico's house. He was pleased to see me again. He poured a question at me "Have you visited the Hermetic Library in Amsterdam?"

"I decided to go next year, Nico."

"Why next year? Why not now? You are already here, Ingrid! Phone them, make reservations and spend one more day in Holland!"

"Nico, I already decided to come back next year."

Nico realized that my mind was already made up about it. He couldn't possibly know the real reason. I had no money left. I could only get to the Schiphol airport for my flight. We parted in a cordial way and I promised to keep in touch.

The rain subsided. I slowed down in my walk, trying to feel the energy of the city and my heart's connection to it. In two more days I was to leave Europe for Canada. I began to miss my children to whom I phoned a few times. Monica looked after everything. All was well. The children's fathers fortunately lived in the same city and had a regular access to them.

Madame De Schryver saved a lunch for me. She was a true mother: caring, thoughtful. At last, I had a privacy in Jacob's room to look into my Den Alchemist magazine. It was published by a group called Parcifal. Among the contributing writers was Jan Snijder and Hermes. Who was this Hermes? Quickly I found the page with an article called Totaal Liefdesgeluk. From my limited German I understood the meaning: Love's Total Delight. I read the article written in Flemish. I understood every word of it. I felt every line in my Soul. I knew the writer's feelings. I knew him. Who is he who signs by the name of Hermes? He could not be Trismegistus, the trice initiated one. He is someone who lives in these times and dares to use the pen name Hermes. Could he be the one I am seeking?

My heart was racing. I rushed downstairs to phone Nico. He didn't know him. He suggested I get in touch with the bookstore owner and ask him.

Jan might know about this Hermes! I phoned Jan. He didn't know him either. He said that no one knows who he is in real life. He also recommended to ask the bookstore owner.

I phoned Del Alchemist. The kind lady clerk gave me the name of the owner so I could drop off the letter for him with my request. I did it that same afternoon. I left my Canadian connection in it and De Schryver's phone number, just in case.

M y s t i c a l   M a r r i a g e

Jacob picked me up in the morning to take me to a small town called Lier. It was a special place with particular architecture and a charming convent. We listened to the musical clock on the main square, bought some typical Lier pastries, then went to taste more of them in a nearby restaurant. I remembered Marc once telling me that his family lived in Lier for some time.

Jacob had chosen the restaurant. He said he had something to show me there After we ordered our goodies he led me into a small room joined to the dining room. There was a poster with topless women, each of them carrying an oil lamp. Jacob liked the way the artist introduced one of the mysteries to modern man. When we were enjoying the pastries, he asked me, "What do you think about the picture, Ingrid?"

"Weary looking virgins with oil in their lamps," I answered impartially.

"They don't look like virgins to me! They look experienced in every walk of life," said Jacob, waiting for my more passionate input.

Finally, I was to satisfy his expectation.

"Naturally, Jacob. How could they gather the oil for their lamps, otherwise? Only by immersion in real life it is possible, by living it, not escaping it. We don't find it in convents, or monasteries, or by meditating on top of a mountain. I would like to see all those self-righteous men and women to assume the daily responsibilities of today's most of people's lives. Would they be functional, would they have enough compassion and faith to continue the next day, or would they rather retreat into their 'peace'?"

Jacob stopped tasting pastries, looked at me with that familiar spark in his eyes, endulging in the fire of my words. "God really took your heart into His, Ingrid. He needs workers like yourself, He needs that extension of Himself. Your lamp was lit when you have met your Groom, your Comforter."

The pastries had no more taste in my mouth. The first bite was delicious, but our conversation had taken me to another plane. I was back on the street of Santiago, seeing my beloved, feeling the outpouring love from his eyes. The ineffable longing for his return into my life brought sorrow into my heart and tears into my eyes. Jacob passed me his soft napkin, so I could wipe them off. My internal clown uplifted the mood by a deliberately staged louder blow of my nose. We laughed for a brief moment.

"Except, Jacob, I walked away from my Marriage. Instead of partaking of the Heavenly Meal, I walked away. Maybe, I didn't have enough oil to last me through the Feast, or, wasn't pure enough to be a Virgin Bride. I don't think I did well. I went for more oil, but when I returned, He was not there anymore. If you know the story of the Lord's Brides, I was the fallen one."

Jacob placed his loving hand over mine, which was playing with my clean napkin, folding it into a small square.

"When you met your Groom, you were placed into another World. It cannot be measured by time. What makes you believe that there was some nuptial experience to follow? Your Marriage took place in your heart. You had your wedding night and conceived a child. You had your Immaculate Conception, Ingrid! Do you understand me?"

"Jacob, you are an exceptional catholic priest. Where does your Wisdom come from?"

"From you, my Sister. Being with you and around you changes my perception. You are the catalyst. Thank you!"

There was no need to say more. We had shared with each other what had to be said and heard. When there is balance and harmony, the Truth is always present. Every question has its answer, or otherwise, there is no question.

That day was a sweet day. When we returned to Berchem, Jacob's parents invited us for Belgian waffles with berries and cream. In the late evening I tried to play their piano which was very much out of tune. Nobody had played it for years. I picked a few tunes and ended with Ombra Mai Fu, sending the sound waves toward my Groom, wherever He was. The next day I was to part with this special family, their city, country, and our continent. I knew that I'd be back.

At the Schiphol airport I was browsing around the duty free shops, observing the crowd of shoppers and travelers. I've seen more tall and slender men here than in Canada. Many of them had the same body type as my beloved. Definitely, I was to be back next year.

My children were glad I was back. Monica did an excellent job with the children, household, and money. She actually saved thirty dollars for me, knowing, I would return broke.

Hanna came within days to see photos from Europe and spent hours on the phone with me, listening to my adventures. She was astonished about the flow of the events, about people I've met. She was hopeful that I might hear from the mysterious Hermes, but strongly believed that I'll hear from Frank.

Ray was quite detached from my story and I began to feel some negativity from him. It didn't bother me. I still considered him to be a good friend, but the gap between us was growing wider. He was one of those meditators avoiding real life. He preferred to live in the unreality of his own mind creation. I wondered who was more daring. Him or I? We were both chasing our vision. My subject in my reality was tangible. His subject was tangible in his reality. In a sense, we were doing the same, except, on different planes. The best is to wait for our harvest and its fruit.

Toward the end of July I was phoned about an audition for a new season. It was recommended that I try for a solo in Bach's BWV 140 Wachet Auf. I picked up the score and the tape with the cantata. Wachet Auf means Beware. It is a message to maidens, the Brides of the Christ, to be ready with an oil in their lamps for his coming to the wedding feast. Prior to the part I was to practice was a Recitativo No.5 with a male voice introducing Duet No.3. At the end of Recitativo a kiss on the right cheek is mentioned. The pelican kissed me twice on the right cheek! I read the words in the Duet. The base voice is of the Bridegroom, soprano is that of the Bride. She asks her Saviour when he was coming and he keeps on answering that He was coming. She was waiting for Him with the lit up oil lamp. He was opening the bridal chamber for the heavenly feast, inviting her. She says "Come, Jesus" and he answers "I am coming to the Feast." "Come, my Saviour, I am waiting with the lit up oil lamp." The duet is a continuous dialogue of the Noble Couple and the melody reflects the motif. I fell in love with the piece.

Auditions were held in the Lutheran Church. Many singers who were known and unknown to me came to give it a chance. Hanna came along to give me a support.

My name was called. The base was a young singer. I took a comfortable standing position and set my mind in the mood. As I began to sing, I could see myself face to face with my beloved on the street of Santiago, having a dialogue with him. He opened a door behind him and invites me into a Bridal Chamber. I place my lamp on the round table and drink from the cup he offered me. I felt every word and the tune throughout my body. I realized that it was over when the director called the next person.

I sat down next to Hanna. She squeezes my hand, saying "You are a hell of a singer! It was beautiful! I had chills all over my back, I could feel the tingle along my spine. I bet you'll get the part!"

We waited a little longer and then quietly left.

This whole cantata was about the Mystical Marriage. Even though I didn't get to sing the solo at the performance, I enjoyed being a chorister and one of many Maidens.

J. S. Bach was big on mysteries. Most of his works are in German, but I was enriched by singing his Mass B minor, that is written in Latin. Something special happened to me during one of the rehearsals. In the Resurrection part some absolutely gorgeous music accompanies the words "He ascended to Heaven to sit at the right hand of the Father". I began to grow bigger and bigger, coming out of my seat and rising. Quickly I grabbed the seat, checking around if anyone noticed anything. Luckily, I was in the last row and everyone was too busy reading the score. Likely, no one would notice it. It was an out of body experience. I began to recognize a B minor scale as being in resonance with the Earth' frequency. Our bodies must be in tune with that frequency.

101

Interestingly, Frank lived on the Bach Street. I wrote him twice, but had not received any answer from him yet.

Bach's music brought me a great joy into my life and led me into meeting Archon.

Archon

My family's survival was challenged. I worked hard on generating a business with products I had for sale. I had some shows booked prior to Christmas but was getting stressed about the upcoming goods and services tax. Regardless of people's opposition to it, our government chose to test our patience anyway. It was implemented and people stopped buying what they could do without. It destroyed many small businesses and entrepreneurs. Before I returned the product to the company for a refund, I tried to sell some of it for a profit. Our financial situation was critical. I needed help.

In the middle of February '91 I was having a very unusual dream: another phone call, this time from my soul mate Gabriel, whom I met many years ago in Canada at the time of my first divorce. Gabi was from my old country and tried to make a living in Canada as an artist, painting. He was very gifted. In this dream Gabi was instructing me to take a massage course. He said that I'll be able to provide for my family.

This was the third message I received about the healing arts. The first one came when I was between my second and third marriage from another countryman, who was an excellent masseur. He kept on telling me that I would make a very good masseuse and wouldn't have to struggle financially. The second message came directly from a friend of my friend who, for some strange reason, believed that I had the power to heal him. When I put all this together and my need to touch people, which was very natural and spontaneous with me, I decided to inquire about massage courses available. At the registrar of the College they told me that next Monday they are registering for the massage programme. I went with my only eighty dollars, hoping, that the rest can be paid with postdated cheques. It wasn't possible, but they agreed to reserve my registration for the day if I come up with the rest of the payment. I phoned Eduardo and a couple of other friends. They loaned me the money and I was anxiously waiting for my classes to start.

We had a very good teacher and soon I realized that this work was 'my cup of tea'. I loved it and was very good at it. My health was affected by a previous stress, but the channeling of the healing energy helped me. I was radiant again and could do with five hours of sleep.

One evening I organized a viewing of a very interesting video at my place. A friend recommended I call Trevor, who was interested in the subject. He came. At the door I recognized him from the auditions. He was tall, strong, and very handsome.

I mentioned our upcoming concert to the group and sold a couple of tickets. Trevor didn't buy any, but kept on observing me and asked me why I sing Bach and what else I was doing. He also asked me about languages I speak.

The next day Trevor phoned me and wanted to chat. We had a lot in common. I accepted an invitation to a dinner he was to prepare himself.

We had a good talk about many areas of life and began to appreciate each other's company. Trevor claimed that he had a gift of automatic writing and was called by the name of Archon. When I asked him who calls him that way, he had a vague explanation, but showed me some of his writings. He said that he knew that I was coming into his life ten years ago. As a matter of fact, he showed me a paper he wrote at that time describing me, my physiology, characteristics, talents, skills, languages spoken, and I was to sing Bach's music. He played to me a tape where an identical voice to mine was singing. He had another two copies of the paper with his friends for the last ten years. I checked with one of them. It was true. I went to see her. She was a herbalist. She told me that Trevor could not progress in his development without me and that I was to show him the way and the opportunity to grow. She also said that Trevor had only male reincarnations. Everything else I was willing to accept as a possibility, but this was totally ridiculous. There was no way to prove it anyway. He was very masculine, but had no problems with woman's chores, or would he have a macho personality. In any case, I found the whole story entertaining and interesting enough to keep on seeing Trevor regularly. He hoped for a relationship. I told him about my beloved to whom I was committed. On the next date Trevor passed me some channeled material to read. It said that my beloved was on another plane of consciousness and had no incarnation. I didn't believe it and, as a matter of fact, I was upset that Trevor used his 'gift' to manipulate me. I stopped seeing him. He kept on trying to get me back into his life, having more channeled writings for me. I told him he was posessed. Then he asked me for help. I went. I used a technique similar to Reiki on him, but it comes very naturally with feeling. Trevor felt fantastic after, but the next day he got very ill. He asked me for help again. When I went to his place and embraced him, a gray cold energy exits through his head, causing his body to shiver for a moment. Trevor stands before me radiant, with blue eyes I've never seen on him. He was absolutely gorgeous. He believed that I liberated him from some dark entity and that I came to his life to heal him. He quit his automatic writing. Slowly, but surely, we were falling in love with each other. It created a conflict within me, but I had to remind myself of experiencing life fully in the given moment and, of the beingness in every breath we take. I practiced it in my massages, but had to learn to practice it in my own life. It was easy to love Trevor. He was a beautiful specimen of manhood and, he adored me. Shortly after he asked me to marry him. I said I'll think about it. I had to consider consequences. I felt I would betray my beloved, whose name and where abouts I didn't have. I chose to test the situation. I introduced Trevor to my children. None of them felt comfortable with him. Monica was with us at Easter, so she met him. Andrew was afraid of him. Sometimes children fear a new family member for selfish reasons, so I decided to give it time. I continued seeing Trevor, but analyzed the situation.

Monica was graduating from Bible College, so, I had to make a trip to Swift Current. Trevor wanted to come along. Monica specified that she doesn't want him to come. "I don't feel comfortable around him", she said to me. "I don't know what it is, Mom, but be careful, please...."

Over the years I learned to respect my children's feedback. They can be very intuitive. I went by myself.

Trevor expected me with a home made meal on my return He showed me a writing he said he had to do for me. He said it came from an entity called Dorma. I knew from Trevor that he doesn't hear voices. He perceives messages on the vibrational feeling level. Part of the message was in a strange language. How could Trevor possibly come up with something like that? The message said that Ingrid would recognize the language, but Trevor would not. My intuition suggested that it was Sanskrit. It was phonetically written.

Surely enough, we had an argument over a little thing, just like the message said. I left Trevor's house, taking the writing with me. He gave it to me. I remembered thoughts I had on my return from Swift Current. Something in my heart kept saying that my beloved was in incarnation and that I had to choose the direction I was to take. The intense love for my beloved was coming back and I knew that I had to break up with Trevor. It was almost happening.

I phoned the university and asked the Sanskrit professor about the words in the message. They were almost identical with the slight exception. The meaning was deep, significant, and personal. It was an instruction to me.

I didn't want to tell Trevor about it. He would go back to his channeling and I felt that it was a cause of his problem. I visited with him though. He was very negative and was sending me away. His eye and skin colour had changed. His voice was slightly subdued. I offered help. He said I'd better help myself, that I was totally lost with my christianity and christian archetypes. I left, but visited with his lady friend, the herbalist. She was very concerned about him and told me more about his past history. She was not happy about his channeling either. She asked if I loved him enough to exorcise him, if he asked for help. He never asked.

I saw Trevor one more time on one very nurturing lecture. The presenter was a true mystic. She spoke about the gnostic writings in the collection called The Nag Hammadí Library. She quoted some lines. It was powerful. Among chapters was one on Archons. Trevor and I looked at each other instantly. That was the last eye to eye contact we had.

I have no idea what Trevor had done with the information, but I called the Hermetic Library in Amsterdam, asking about Archons. They said that there is a chapter on them in The Nag Hammadí book. They gave me the ISBN number of the book so I could order it. They also offered me information on their library. When I asked who the owner was, the secretary said that Mr. Josef Ritman. There was a moment of silence. I burned with curiosity. I gave them my address and anxiously waited for information they offered to send me.

The same day I went to a book store to place an order for the gnostic gospels. To my surprise, they had two copies of the book in the store but nobody touched them yet. I bought both of them. One for me and one for Trevor.

As soon as I got to my car, I scanned the Table of Contents. On page 161 there was The Hipostasis of the Archons. At home I began to read. I was astonished. They are called Rulers and have a different origin of creation than most of us earthlings. The chapter goes back to Genesis and explains Archons as androgynous, but in male bodies. Their mission here is over once they "Defile the Virgins of the World." They can never incarnate the Soul.

I never gave the book to Trevor. I just couldn't do it to him. In the later half of summer he phoned me, asking forgiveness. He claimed that he had no memory of what transpired betweem us. He asked if we can start all over again. At this point I told him that his writing was in Sanskrit and the message was very meaningful to me. I thanked him for it but assured him that our paths had already crossed and we each must go ahead and pursue our own journey.

P e l i c a n

The graduation from the Relaxation Massage course was over. Some of the people I knew were willing to give me a chance to practice on them. They paid me for my service and some of them came back. I decided to continue with my training and to save my earnings for the course.

I spent most of the summer days around my children, doing nature walks to the nearby hilly natural park. Nose Hill Park is the home of many birds, rabbits, deer, and coyottes. Andrew enjoyed communicating with a falcon that nested in a tall tree. He and Maria liked to throw pebbles into a small pond nearby, and to hide in the tall grass around it. I enjoyed searching for wild flowers which had grown there in abundance. Some areas around the pond were too humid and there I found a batch of clovers. I thought of the good luck a four-leaved clover brings and, passing my hand over the batch, I found several four-leaved clovers. I picked them, dried them in my books and, with the exception of one, I gave the other ones away to share the good luck.

As soon as the mail was delivered, I picked it up. Letters from Jacob were coming regularly. Christian wrote less, knowing that I found my way. I never received any mail from Frank, even though I sent him a card and a letter with my address.

On the third anniversary of the encounter with my beloved came a large white envelope with an emblem of a pelican. It was from the Bibliotheca Philosophica Hermetica, located on Bloemgracht 19, in Amsterdam. I received my information from the library that Nico wanted me to visit. Before opening the envelope, I inspect the emblem. The pelican was feeding three young, instead of two. All the birds were standing in a moon crescent that was on top of a cube with symbols of Alpha and Omega. Above the pelican's head there was a sun with seven rays. Oval emblem was lined by the green snake biting on its own tail The emblem reflected my 'dream experience' I had on September 12th, 1988, when the pelican kissed me twice on the right cheek! Bloemgracht means the 'canal of flowers'. In my dream I saw a canal and smelled flowers from every direction. Was my beloved in this library, or was he Josef Ritman himself? I was thrilled. I had no more patience. Action was my only solution. I was so close to my goal!

The pelican and the dream was my key, so was a library and a name ending with "man". The name Josef came across several times, so did Holland.

Mr. Ritman received from me a letter that would melt a rock. In turn I received an invitation to the library, when I visit Holland. This wasn't good enough. I needed to know how Mr. Ritman looks like. I must had intimidated the curator with my question on Mr. Ritman's height, but when I asked who designed the emblem for the library, I was given a name of one gentleman from Antwerp. The curator was kind enough to give me his phone number.

The Belgian designer explained that the symbol was very old and that he was hired to do the artwork. I figured that he must had met all people working in the library, so I asked about a tall man of certain features I specified. He immediately named a nephew of Mr. Ritman, who was in his forties. Within minutes I had his address and the phone numbers of people who could give me more information. I had to plan long distance phone calls with budget on mind.

For the first time I celebrated my birthday. I was forty five! Marc, Ray and Hanna came. Marc gave me a bouquet of orchids, Ray gave me a digital alarm clock and a set of Tarot cards. Hanna had a marble sculpture of Jesus' bust and a cake she called 'the sex in the pan' for me. It was so scrumptuously delicious, it almost sucked my glands out. I asked Ray why he chose the gift he gave me. He felt it was time for me to look at the symbolism of Tarot. He had deliberately chosen a celtic deck instead of the design by Aleister Crowley that I liked. Since I never planned on getting Tarot cards, it became a special gift.

Our celebration was absolutely lovely. We nibbled on many goodies. Ray happened to eat a lot, which was very unusual for him. He's been a vegetarian for ages and practiced ascetism in everything. Then I noticed that he's been going bathroom frequently, so I asked him if he was feeling all right. He replied that he felt great and enjoyed what I prepared.

Later on in the evening we happened to lead our conversation into my quest. All my close friends knew about my search and liked to keep up with the latest news, since there was always something happening. Ray shared with us a result of one of his meditations on Ritman Library. He said that Josef was a stocky short man. He did some follow up work in opening up the communication between me and him.Obviously, my beloved was someone else and I was to find out soon.

A few days after my birthday I received some registered mail from the Library. In it was a Dutch publication called Bres 103 with a long article on the library, many illustrations from the original manuscripts, and a picture of the emblem with the explanation of its symbolism. Fortunately Marc translated most of it. I was ecstatic! My dream was more than a dream. I was truly blessed by uniting with my Soul. At the age of forty-two I united with my twin soul and my own Soul! If a pelican feeding two young in christian symbolism represents Christ, what does a pelican feeding three young represent in hermetic symbolism? Why did I think that He was my beloved?

I had to keep communication lines busy, sending questions, expecting answers. Aaron would not agree with me. He would say that I push too much, not allowing the natural enfoldment. Personally, I felt I had nothing to lose if I write to Adriaan, Mr. Ritman's nephew. I sent him a short letter stating that I'll be visiting library next summer and would like to get in touch with him. I included my address and phone number. Now, I had three unanswered letters I sent to Frank, Hermes, and Adriaan.

Guides

In October Ray asked me to pick up a Tarot Guide book he ordered for me. He lived in a high rise apartment building and brought the book for me to the main door. I was in a hurry.

When I saw Ray, a shiver ran down my back. His upright posture was changed into the posture of an old man, with a curved back. His complexion had an unhealthy colour and his eyes lost their spark. Instantly, the word cancer came to my mind. I asked Ray if he was feeling alright. He answered that recently he had a cold. I gave him a hug that he needed and left. I shared my concern with Hanna. We prayed for him and I began to phone him frequently, checking on him. I had to create a reason for phoning him. Tarot symbolism was a perfect excuse. One day Ray sent me a letter about his work done on my behalf. When I asked him why he'd done it, he claimed that his guides insisted.

"Who are your guides, Ray?" I asked. I felt mistrust.

"They're angels. You know that I work with angels, Ingrid!"

"Angels do not interfere, Ray! Who are your guides?" I demanded a much clearer explanation.

"Ingrid, I already told you! They're angels!" Ray was becoming upset about my questions.

"What are their names, then?"

"Hugel, Jungel... and others," Ray answered, having already gained his calm.

"How about Huge Jungle? Listen Ray, I don't like your angels! Just because their names end with EL, it doesn't make them angels yet. Remember, angels do not interfere! I didn't ask you, or them, to get involved in my case!"

"Actually, Ingrid, they would like to work with you."

"Since they're your friends, tell them to stay out of my life and if you consent, tell them to stay out of your life, for your sake!" I was really heated up. My gut feeling was so strong behind my words.

"What are you talking about, Ingrid? I worked with them for years! They are angels!"

"Bullshit! They are those rotten dark entities feeding on the ambitious spiritual seekers, who are anxiously waiting for some apparition from the other side and who are gullible because they lack experience. They are sucking energy out of you! Don't you see it, Ray?"

"I've never heard you speaking in this way, Ingrid! What's the matter with you?"

"Look, Ray, don't try to sell me your angels. You created them, you deal with them. But I don't like what they're doing to you. They are taking your life force!"

"They are helping me!"

"To what? Keeping you busy writing, so you cannot have any rest and decent sleep, making you believe that your work has value. They've done a good number on you, Ray!"

Surprisingly, Ray was not upset about my words. He just asked me if there was something else about the Tarot symbolism I wanted to know. I had no more questions. I wished him peace and hung up the phone. I became more concerned about his health. I felt there was a trade between him and his guides. He used their energy first, now they came back for it. In a sense, they became an extension of his being, and him, being a source of energy for them.

I had no regrets about what I said to Ray. It came from my being that reveres divinity in all life, but uses discernment when necessary. I cared for Ray. I'd known him for the last twelve years. The time had come that I had to detach from him and allow him to learn from his own choices. I phoned less. Sometimes no one answered the phone. Surprisingly, it didn't bother me.

Not much had changed in my family's activities. Monica worked in Swift Current, Joe and Jean were in high school. I kept on driving the children to school and going for my classes on some weekdays. My musical activities hadn't changed either. Singing was my daily remedy and the piano was a pleasant companion. Income was still scarse, so I kept our spendings low. We were getting by, just barely surviving. Some things had to change. I changed my expectations and began to plan another trip to Europe for the following summer.

Exactly on Monica's birthday the phone rang when I was already leaving to take the children to school. I picked it up. I heard the familiar beeps of a long distance call. An operator speaking in Spanish asked for me. A person to person call from Spain. Being in a hurry I had little patience. I asked her who was calling and she told me that Mr. ...... I had never heard this name and told her that I don't know this person and that it must be an error. She asked for my name again and insisted that the caller wanted to speak with me. I was hanging up when I heard a familiar male voice that spoke to me a few times giving me information about my spiritual direction. I hung up. At that instant I realized what I'd done, lifted the receiver, but the line was gone. I didn't even capture what the voice was saying. I rushed to the car to make it to the school on time. Did I ever regret my impatience and spontaneity. This could had been the call I awaited for over three years! I hoped that he'd call back. Hanna was very disappointed in me. She believed that it was a call from my beloved.

He didn't call back. I was learning from my mistake - a big mistake. Someone connected to me was in Spain. Could that be Hermes? Time would tell.

Hanna phoned me about a dream she had about me. She described the room as a European residence where someone was just moving in or out. There was only a chesterfield. A man who looked very much like Ray, but had much lovelier features and a taller figure, was enchanted by what I was saying to him.

She described him in detail, sitting on the sofa, listening to every word I was saying. Him and I were extremely happy and radiant.

"Hanna," I interrupted, "did I ever tell you that my beloved looks like a better version of Ray?"

"No, never..., does he, really?"

"Yes, very much so. You saw my beloved!"

"He is very much in love with you, Ingrid. His face was glowing. He was totally taken by you!"

"He might be in Europe afterall! I am going next summer. I have to go!"

"I can clearly see that. Things will work out for you, you'll see!" Hanna assured me.

Then we talked about Ray. I hadn't been able to reach him for a week now, so I began on phoning several times a day. A few days later I went to his apartment building and asked the manager about him. He said that Ray was taken to the hospital a few days ago. The first hospital I phoned admitted him. When I told them that I was Ray's close friend, they had his doctor to phone me back. I was the only person asking about Ray. They thought he had no relatives. The doctor already operated on Ray's prostate. It was cancer and it metastasized. He said that Ray's heart was very weak I went to see Ray that same afternoon. He looked terribly pale, tubes in his nose, an IV piercing his thin arm. I pretended he looked fine to me.

"How did you find out?" he asked.

"The building manager told me. What's happening?"

"They want to give me a blood transfusion.", Ray answered.

"Why is that?"

"I am weak. But I have to go through this. Angels told me that I'll go through transformation. This is the beginning."

"Like Lazarus?" Ray didn't respond "Well," I continued, "Christmas starts next week, Easter is around the corner. Many things can happen. What do you think?"

"I think angels are testing me," Ray answered softly.

There was no emotion attached to his words. All of a sudden I realized that he never showed any. He was fully capable of using correct words to say something nice, but it lacked depth. I was looking at a dying man, who denied his heart and sexuality, the exact areas of illness. He lived in his head where all mental processes took place, where he created a scenario of his drama. He decapitated himself from his own body. In order to heal himself he was to connect to his body, flood it with feelings of love and acceptance.

"Can I come to visit you again? What can I do for you?" I asked.

"You have your own family, Ingrid. Do not worry about me. Angels are looking after me."

"Ray, send them to hell. Exactly where they belong. You don't need them. You need to find yourself. Christmas is coming, Advent is here."

"I'll prove my resurrection. You'll see!"

"That's ego stuff, Ray. You need to prove nothing. Just connect to the innocence of the child in you, find it in the manger of humility among the creatures of the Earth!"

Ray kept silent. We parted. His doctor was on duty. He was in his late thirties and was generous with information. They wrote my name and phone number on Ray's file, so I could be notified about any change.

Our home was already decorated for Christmas and I had my baking done. The children were about to have holidays and Monica was to come. A care parcel from my mother came with some gifts and a large box of chocolate figurines we traditionally hang on our Christmas tree. Among the gifts were two towels with initials in the pattern. They were an A and a D. My Mom explained in the letter that she tried several stores to get initials of my whole family, but after finding many with A's they had only one with a D. She bought it anyway.

I visited Ray in the hospital and brought him some of our goodies and a Christmas card. It was my opportunity to uplift him. I succeeded. The words I'd written were directed to his heart. Ray was in a good mood. He looked rosier after receiving someone else's blood. I came back on boxing day. He hoped to be released from the hospital soon.

I kept on coming to see him almost daily before New Year's Eve. The doctor wanted him to try chemotherapy, but Ray was not interested. Ray asked for my opinion. I told him he should do what he feels is right for him. The next day he was released. I made sure he had a food supply in his home and that he was safe being by himself. He enjoyed the attention. We talked about life. Ray had regrets. He said that without a family old age is sad. I wondered if he would say anything like it while being healthy. I doubted. I remained a good friend and did my best to assist him. Between my family, work, and music, I could come to his place only three times a week and help as much as I could. He was not getting better, but at least stopped talking about his angels and I believed that he quit with them.

Ray looked for healing from another level. He wouldn't take Essiac herbal extract, which was known to 'flush' cancer out of the system, but he called a Chinese psychic, who had some interesting suggestions and, after dowsing Ray's apartment, he said that it was full of dark energy. A shopping list suggested two Chinese 'good luck' signs, chimes by the door and windows, and vertical blinds. Some changes had to be done in the apartment and Ray had to give away his beautiful ivy plants and a huge fig tree. They were apparently taking energy away from him. They all did well in my home. Ray loved his plants and sometimes asked me how they were doing. I gave him a regular report on them.

My classes started again and I had to take on another part-time job. I became a waitress two days a week. I had hardly any time to see Ray. He agreed to a home care provider and 'meals on wheels'.

One day a friend came over to my place and complimented on the botany of my home but rebukes me for not watering one ivy.

"What are you talking about?" I told her. "I water regularly. Don't you see?"

She touched the soil. It was humid but the ivy was completely dry, as if life left it. Every leaf was dark green, but dried. Immediately a thought of Ray came to my mind. Is he all right?

I dialed his number right away. No answer. I dialed many more times and got no answer. I phoned the hospital. He was admitted again. He actually called an ambulance the last night. He had problems with breathing and was afraid that he would die.

This ivy was his favourite and decorated a wall in his place ever since I'd known him. He used to say that plants are connected to humans on the etheric plane and have a spirit to heal them. At that time he told me about homeopathic remedies and herbalism. The ivy was fully alive on the previous day. It must had been connected to Ray's crisis. I told him about it during my visit in the hospital. It cheered him up only for a while. A few days later he consented to chemotherapy.

Gnosis

A friend who was aware of my philosophical nature had mentioned a Salvadorian group that offers teachings on Gnosticism for free. He said that Juan was a good teacher and offered to put me in touch with him.

Juan happened to live nearby so we agreed to meet in the beautiful outdoors of Nose Hill Park where his and my children could have some healthy fun together while we talked. Juan had that lively spark in his eyes. He knew nothing about the pelican, but told me about a library that uses the symbol. Then I told him that I was planning on going there in summer. This happened around Easter.

"Well," said Juan, "in this case you'd better view a video I have about this library. It is called "Knowledge of the Heart". It is on Gnosis. Then you can decide whether or not you want to come to our lectures."

"Juan, why is the book of my quest unfolding so easily, page by page?"

"Because you've written it yourself. You already know it. You are just rerunning it in your memory. Do not forget that your body lives in the dimension of time, but your mind lives in timelessness. Your body releases information in time, step by step, page by page. There is a sequence to every event outside and inside you. There are no shortcuts, remember that. You are the actress of your own drama and you are the play-wright. The important people you meet are the co-authors of your comedy, if you wish to call it that way."

Our conversation expanded into the areas of our common interest. I anxiously awaited the next morning when Juan was to drop off the video. In the late evening, when I had some privacy, I began to watch. It started on the history of the Nag Hammadí Library and continued into present day gnosticism and its varied practices.

The third part was on the Hermetic Library. Mr. Ritman was a shorter, stocky man, just like Ray said. The library's curator was an archetypal man. I could clearly see that I was to visit a true treasure of philosophical literature. The library was financed by Mr. Ritman's company called Ster, which means Star. A tremendous vision and purpose must had guided this man, who accomplished so much. Positively, I was to be privileged by visiting it and reading another page of my comedy.

A ' d a m

My part-time job paid for my charter flight to Europe. Due to working for someone else I qualified for a credit card. A neighbour was offering me money for my car. Between Jean, summer camp, and their father, Maria and Andrew were to be taken care of and, I was free to go. I could afford the trip afterall!

Ray's doctor assured me that Ray was going to be around for at least several months and wished me a good trip. Hanna reminded me to keep a journal and to tell her about every detail when I'd return. Jacob was excited about seeing me again. I had decided to phone Jan and Nico once I was in Europe.

Prior to leaving I went to a naturopath for advice on what to take with me as preventive remedies. When she found out that I was a massage therapist, she tried to recruit me to work in her clinic. I told her that I'd consider after my trip. She was a lovely Jewish lady and we both spoke Russian. She promised she'd teach me everything she knew if I come to work with her.

The neighbour, who bought my car, drove me to the airport. I sat down in the waiting area a couple seats away from the nearest person. His ears were plugged with earphones, listening to his CD player. In a short moment he took off the earphones and apologized for loud music.

"Actually, I didn't hear anything," I told him. "What are you listening to?" I asked, knowing that he wanted to start a conversation.

"It is my favourite music: Handel."

"You must like baroque music, then!"

"All of it, but Handel's is special."

"I know what you mean. Everyone loves his Messiah. What were you listening to, tell me!"

"Guess!" he challenged me.

"Israel in Egypt? Water Music?"

"Close... guess again. He had a mischievous smile. He was about my age, quite good looking. He seemed familiar to me.

"Royal Fireworks?"

"You're getting closer! Guess again!" He was sitting next to me by now, looking straight into my eyes, almost suggesting the name of Handel's composition.

"I give in. I don't know. Help me!"

"Water, Fire... try!"

I felt almost intimidated. I must had shown a surrender in my eyes.

"Alchemist!" he exclaimed.

"I didn't know that anyone composed The Alchemist!" Suddenly, I remembered the Flemisch term for a bookstore in Antwerp. "There is a Boek-Handel Den Alchemist in Antwerpen, did you know that?"

"My favourite one is in Amsterdam, called Arcanum," he answered immediately.

"My name is Ingrid," I shook his hand in introduction.

"I am Bertus. Nice to meet you."

I just remembered him. "You know Marc and his wife! We were introduced once, remember? It was in Banff!"

Bert remembered, but we didn't recognize each other at first. He was going to visit his children in Holland and decide about his family's future. I told him I was going to the Hermetic Library.

We had to get ready for the security check. We saw each other twice briefly during the flight. We each had our own destination. He happened to point mine out to me.

Walking with luggage in a European city is not much fun. It didn't really matter where I was to stay the first night, as long as they would accept the VISA card. I found a lovely hotel on the main street near the Centraal Station. I was within walking distance to the library, a direct way by the Royal Palace. A little city map, that folded into the shape of a tulip, was worth a picture more than a thousand words.

Eager to take a shower and to slip into comfortable clothes before the rehearsal of my first visit to the place where the pelican had guided me, I opened a right panel of the curtain to let some daylight in and see who the neighbours across the street were. I saw before my eyes a sign with the large capital letters KING. When I opened the left curtain panel, I read BURGER. It was the Burger King in Amsterdam. I shut the left panel. I could not afford a Whopper anyway - the price was triple the Canadian one. When I was ready to leave, passing over the threshold of the door, I looked back at the KING, that would faithfully await my return.

In the center of A'dam (the Dutch short version for Amsterdam) there was lots of activity. Pedestrians, traffic, tramways, bicycles, red lights, green lights, and hardly any yellow. The words of my mother from my early childhood echoed in my memory once again. Each time I was leaving our house, she reminded me to look left and right before I set foot off the sidewalk. Watch for those cars, she always said. We lived at a busy intersection and witnessed some ugly accidents over the years.

Ten minutes later, I was coming nearer Westerkirk by Prinsengracht. I had to cross one more bridge, turn the corner, and there was Bloemstraat, parallel to Bloemgracht. This was a district called Jordaan. I walk by the Ster company that had window shutters in the shape of tulips. This company financed the Library's activities. Now I am coming to Bloemgracht. The sound of the street noises, the humid air, the feeling of cobble stones under my soles, and, myself, standing by the canal, looking at the houses across the street. Exactly the same experience I had on the 12th of September, 1988! Where was my pelican? I looked around, toward my right, up to the sky. No bird was flying, no man was walking toward me. I was standing there alone, perhaps being observed by someone behind a crochet curtain through the immaculately washed windows. The houses on the other side of the canal looked the same, but one of them, with the number 19, had the coloured emblem of a pelican and the written words IN DE PELIKAAN right above the door. Tomorrow I'd enter through that door, into the pelican's heart. A great joy poured over me. I was truly living my comedy!

Anxious to turn to the next page, I was inspecting my immediate environment. A pub, an antique shop, and a bridge. This bridge had the name Twelve Lilies! Maybe the next one would be Orchids, or Roses. Well, the canal is called Flowers.

I must had been dreaming too much. An impatient driver honked at me right behind my heels. I quickly jumped to the side, to share the space with trees... and... dog droppings. I stepped into one. Just one more fragrance on the Bloemgracht and a reminder of reality.

Now keeping more to the side, I enjoyed myself, walking through the street of my dreams. I noticed that a couple of houses were offering bed and breakfast. I inquired. There was no privacy in the first one. It was far too modest for the price. No, this couldn't be in my play. I asked in the other one. This one was in my script. It offered an actual apartment with all conveniences. The price was right! I prepayed and arranged with the owner for the next morning. Now I knew where I'd be sleeping, where I'd be going, but I had no idea what was ahead of me. My threedimensional body needed rest and to become one with the regenerated mind toward the morning.

I could hardly wait to get my act together to please the director and the audience. I had no stage fright, I kept calm, trusting myself. I couldn't possibly forget or skip any of my lines. The stage was ready and I continued with my comedy.

In De Pelikaan house with the emblem in the center.

PART THREE

Ingrid Heller

The Divine Comedy
by Dante

My sleep was interrupted by numerous chimes of the Royal Palace's clock. When my northamerican timed body had finally fallen asleep, it was awakened by the street noises. I got up and opened the right panel of the drapes, to be welcomed by the KING. I gathered my belongings, locked the door, paid my bill, and on foot proceeded in the direction of Jordaan.

My large suitcase was injured on the bumpy cobble stones, and at each crossing, yet, made it on three wheels to our 'new temporary home', maintaining its balance with my support.

I had an actual apartment. The bedroom with two single beds attached to each other had a bathroom, and next to it there was a small kitchen where I could prepare my meals. A phone was available by the bedside. On the canal view side there was a spacious fully furnished living room with a television. I could see from my window the house No. 19!

I phoned the library to confirm my reservation. They reminded me that I was to go to Bloemstraat No. 15. When I asked why, they explained that it was the actual location of the library, yet their mail was arriving to Bloemgracht 19.

I was getting ready for my 'date'. The landlord of the apartment knew Ritman's family well and emphasized that this library was the only one of its kind, where many people from around the world go to visit and study. He also told me that Mr. Ritman had seven children and by now had several grandchildren. He held a great admiration for him and his family. He wished me a memorable visit.

I rang the doorbell of the library and announced myself into an intercome. The door buzzed open and I entered. Another door made of glass with the carved emblem was opened. A receptionist welcomed me, showed me the study area, and offered a brief tour through the library, introducing me to the various sections. I looked around to find some familiar faces, but none I had met before. The place was very cleverly designed by the Belgian Eric van den Bossche, who gave me some information earlier. The octagonal white table under a pyramid shaped skylight was the common study area. I was to sign in the guest book. I flipped through the pages to find some familiar names. None rang a bell. I found only one address from Canada. It belonged to Arpad Joe, the well known Hungarian conductor. Most of the visitors were Europeans.

I picked a couple of books written by a Bohemian mystic Comenius, who lived in exile in Holland and whom Dutch people treated with reverence. The books were in Czech. The Labyrinth of the World is a famous philosophical text.

Since my childhood I had a fascination for Jan Amos Komenský's work. He truly understood the learning process and its integration into our memory, how to learn other languages with the guidance of this process, using images and their relationships. I would call it super learning.

The Westerkirk's clock stroke twelve times. The library was closing for lunch hour. I went to my apartment and had a light lunch that the landlord left me in my room.

When I returned to the library, the receptionist brought a few books she selected for me. One of them was a treasure. It was full of symbolism used in alchemy and Cabbalah. The other large book had actual pictures of mysteries and archetypes, with explanations in a fine print underneath. I certainly needed several days to go through this material. Page by page, I immersed myself into the symbolism, revealing sacred psychology woven into our spiritual blueprint, taking us into the Microcosm of the Universe within ourselves. I felt gratitude! How many learned individuals and talented artists compiled these works, nurturing the souls of the seekers of Truth, helping them to remember and to be able to transform their truth! Tears of Joy had filled my eyes because... I began to remember. At times, my emotions were too intense and I had to switch to another book for a while. There were so many to choose from!

The library's atmosphere felt sacred. The energy was vibrant. How many other libraries offer an environment like this one? I looked around again and my eyes fixed themselves on two large sculptures of the busts of Lorenzo and Cosimo de Medici, the well known Florentian nobles, who initiated a collection of philosophical writings and sponsored some translations into other languages. Mr. Ritman was doing the same noble work. Florence! I almost forgot! Dante's Divine Comedy! I rushed toward the section with Dante's work. I had several publications to choose from. I pulled out one with drawings by William Blake and another with a picture of Dante on its jacket, the same I'd seen in Domo of Florence. I took them to my seat. For some unusual reason I began to tremble and perspire. I look again at Dante's face which impressed both Verne and I during our honeymoon in Europe. Why are his features so attractive?

I read contents: The Inferno, The Purgatorio, The Paradiso. I skipped reading the first two parts, but looked at all their drawings. Hell and Purgatory were of no attraction to me. The Paradise interested me. I read page by page, every line of every Canto. There was enough material for several days. At some moments I stopped reading and switched to the Book of Symbols. Turning pages I found a beautiful snow white pelican sitting on the tip of a steep rocky mountain top and, underneath, I read the words:

"Under the symbolism of alchemical marriage, medieval philosopher concealed the secret system of spiritual culture whereby they hoped to coordinate the disjecta membra of both the human and social organisms. Society, they maintained, was a threefold structure and had its analogy in the triune constitution of man, for as man consists of spirit, mind and body, so society is made up of the church, the state and the populace. The bigotry of the church, the tyranny of the state and the fury of the mob are the three murderous agencies of society which seek to destroy. The first six days of the Chemical Marriage set forth the processes of philosophical 'creation' through which every organism must pass. The three kings are the threefold spirit of man and consorts the corresponding vehicles of their expression in the lower world. The executioner is the mind, the higher part of which - symbolized by the head - is necessary to the achievement of the philosophical labor. Thus the parts of man - by the alchemists symbolized as planets and elements - when blended together according to a certain Divine formula result in the creation of two philosophic 'babes' which, fed upon the blood of the alchemical bird, become rulers of the world. From an ethical standpoint, the young King and Queen resurrected at the summit of the tower and ensouled by Divine Life represent the forces of Intelligence and Love which must ultimately guide society. Intelligence and Love are the two great ethical luminaries of the world and correspond to enlightened spirit and regenerated body. The bride-groom is reality and the bride the regenerated being who attains perfection by becoming one with reality through a cosmic marriage wherein the mortal part attains immortality by being united with its own immortal Source. In the Hermetic Marriage divine and human consciousness are united in holy wedlock and he in whom this sacred ceremony takes place is designated as 'Knight of the Golden Stone'; he thereby becomes a divine philosophic diamond composed of quintessence of his own sevenfold constitution.

Such is the true interpretation of the mystical process of becoming 'a bride of the Lamb'. The Lamb of God is signified by the Golden Fleece that Jason was forced to win before he could assume his kingship. The flying Lion is illumined will, an absolute prerequisite to the achievement of the Great Work. The walled city represents the sanctuary of wisdom wherein dwell the real rulers of the world - the initiated philosophers."

I sat back and tried to digest what I'd just read. Every word had a significance addressed to a group of certain qualities and I was a member of that family. I couldn't read anymore. Feeling was to take over my mind for a while, retreating itself into the center of my own universe. I paced slowly through the library, reading the titles and authors of book covers, remembering. A powerful contentment embraced me and I felt truly at home.

A doorbell rang again. I looked in the direction of the entrance and recognized a tall archetypal looking man. He was a director. The curator informed him in a soft voice about something, and he looked at me. He went toward his desk and right after walked toward me, welcoming me to the library and adding, "I hope you will enjoy yourself and will find what you're looking for."

I replied,"I already am enjoying myself. I am finding what I was looking for."

I felt this was the right time to give everyone the small gift I brought for them from Canada. The colourful geostones of various shapes and natural designs were received gratefully. The director received a slightly different gift: a bumper sticker saying 'When God Created Man, The Whole World Rested. When God Created Woman, Neither God Nor Man Rested.' He loved it. A simple bumper sticker eased up the tension between us that started one year ago when I asked the questions on Mr. Ritman's physiology. Humour is healing.

I went back to the octagonal table, holding The Divine Comedy. I had to leave the rest to the next day. I had enough spiritual food in me from that day to last me for a long time.

Going back to my apartment, crossing the bridge of Twelve Lilies, feeling an exaltation. How fortunate angels are feeling this way at all times in eternity of a timeless dimension! How does one cross the bridge into their world?

Dante Alighieri holding The Divine Comedy, painting by Domenico di Michelino.

Canto XXV

At the octagonal table I was surrounded by the section on Alchemy. I reached for one book written by Jacob Boehme, in which I found actual recipes on plant alchemy, involving the principles of homeopathy. Metal alchemy boggled my mind - I passed on that section. I felt that the older looking books offered more profound information. They were all in French - an opportunity to practice. "The Elixir of Long Life" interested me. Here I read "Knowledge and Wisdom have to go in pair. Knowledge without Wisdom is pure Ignorance itself." I thought of my friend Ray again. He read hundreds of philosophical books, highlighted important information, always quoted someone else's truth. Being an ascetic, without his complimentary female and catalyst, he had difficulty to incarnate wisdom, which is of feminine nature. And he had no devotion to Divine Mother, which saved many monks on their spiritual path. Further I read "The renaissance is triple: first the renaissance of our mind, secondly that of our heart and the will, third is the renaissance of the body. Many pious men who seek God had regenerated in the spirit and the will, but very few had known about corporal renaissance.". What is the secret behind the regeneration of the body? I was hooked on the subject. Is the aging process natural? Disease could not be in the Creator's plan! Now I had two tasks: to find my beloved and to regenerate my body. What comes first?

My heart desired to find my beloved first. I placed the alchemical texts back into their section and turned to my already chosen Divine Comedy. Paradise! I must find my Adam at Eden! Canto by Canto, I scanned the pages to find something familiar. Dante's knowledge came through a wise Vigil, inspired by Beatrice - Dante's beloved. One powerful encounter with his female transformed the poet into a giant.

I began to read Canto XXV of Paradiso. This one is of the Eighth Sphere: The fixed stars. St. James * The Examination of Hope * St. John the Apostle.

The first six verses drew my emotions into the following: "With a changed voice and with my fleece full grown, I shall return to my baptismal font, a poet, and there assume the laurel crown; for there I entered the faith that lets us grow into God's recognition, and for that faith Peter, as I have said, circled my brow; Thereafter another radiance came forth from the same sphere out of whose joy had come the first flower of Christ's vicarage on earth. And my lady filled with ecstasy and glow ....within the eighth great sphere one glorious great lord greeted the other praising the diet that regales them there. Those glories having greeted and been greeted, turned and stood before me, still and silent, so bright, I turned my eyes away defeated. And Beatrice said, smiling her blessedness: 'Illustrious being in whose chronicle is written our celestial court's largesse, let hope, I pray, be sounded at this height, How often you personified that grace when Jesus gave his chosen three more light!' " The words of Beatrice continue to speak to the poet. From verse 103 I read: "And as a joyous maid will rise and go to join the dance, in honor of the bride and not for any reasons of vain show, so did that radiant splendor, there above, go to the two who danced a joyous reel in fit expression of their burning love, It joined them in the words and melody; and like a bride, immovable and silent, my lady kept her eyes fixed on their glory. 'This is he who lies upon the breast of Our Pelican, and this is He elected from off the cross to make the great behest.'" Verse number 136 led me into the last words of the Canto XXV. "Ah, what a surge of feeling swept my mind when I turned away an instant from such splendor to look at Beatrice, only to find I could not see her with my dazzled eyes, though I stood near her and in Paradise!"

I read the Canto again, and again, feeling its words in my heart. My meeting with my beloved in Santiago had the same qualities. It was another encounter of the poet with his Beatrice, both experiencing a union in Paradise! The eighth sphere of the fixed stars in the city of St. James, in the winter month of Crab, in the year eighty eight! My christed beloved was Dante Alighieri himself! Was I Beatrice, his inspiration and Sophia?

I looked at Dante's picture. My God, it was my beloved's face! The initials D and A from the towels my mother sent me! What are his initials now? Are they the same?

The visiting hours were over at the library. It was Friday. I photocopied the poem and went to my apartment.

As soon as I got in I called Adriaan's house. A lady told me that Adriaan was returning from a two month business trip that night. I was asked to call back later. In the meanwhile I phoned Jacob and Nico and told them that I'd arrive to Antwerp on the fifteenth of July. I had to reserve a few days in the library and be there on the day of the anniversary: the thirteenth of July.

Two hours later I called Adriaan. He knew who I was and asked me when I would like to meet him. I naturally said that soon, that night, if possible. He said that I must be desperate. I told him that I was. We both laughed. He explained that he came to spend three weeks with his family and that they were departing for holidays in the morning, but was open to me and would call me back after discussing it with his wife.

One hour later Adriaan invited me to his home. His schoffeur was already on his way to pick me up.

I was calm. Adriaan couldn't possibly be my beloved, but he could be a very important messenger. He had something for me I needed to hear.

The ride was pleasant, a true sight-seeing tour of the nicer parts of A'dam. We arrived on the cul de sac and entered Adriaan's family's spacious garden. Him, his wife, and other family members shared a peaceful time together around the garden table.

They greeted me very cordially and immediately showed their hospitality. We toasted with wine and got down to the point: why I was guided to the library by the pelican.

Adriaan was a well read man in philosophies and esotericism, having direct access to the great selection of writings. When we got to the discussion on the Great Work, his wife left to assist their children in packing for the trip. Adriaan was a matching description of my beloved, yet, in a slightly different version. He was a balanced person, speaking from a heart, that was enriched with knowledge.

"Ingrid Heller..," he said and smiled mysteriously to himself. "You have an alchemical name. INRI, HELLER, HALLO You were born into the Great Work. Do it, then!"

"I cannot do it without my beloved, Adriaan. I have to find him!"

"Ingrid, Hermes comes to all of us when we are ready. He came to you because you were ready."

"Hermes? He didn't come to me!" I responded, surprised.

"Yes, he did! The Pelican came to you! He showed you the way!"

"The Pelican is Hermes? He is not Christ?" I felt a mystery embracing me and clarity coming my way.

"Our Pelican is Hermes. He came to you, Ingrid. The Great Work is your own work. You can do it with anyone of your own level. You can also do it on your own. The choices are yours."

Great news: more responsibility on my shoulders! Cutting edges, and being without a teacher to whom I could call for councel, is a hell of a path. Doubtlessly, I was fond of adventures and used to a rebirth every morning, not knowing where the next meal was coming from, but learning about the Great Work through my inner guidance and trust, was as challenging as climbing the Mountain by myself under all kinds of weather conditions. I'd better be dressed for the weather! I was ready for the unexpected.

After our chat I parted with Adriaan's wife who was a special woman of noble conduct. Shortly after I was driven back to my apartment by Adriaan himself. He understood me and helped me to feel comfortable about my correspondence to Mr. Ritman, who was on a vacation with his family at that time.

Before going to bed I kept on reading the other translation of Canto XXV. It was more specific in relationship to my encounter with Dante in Santiago. How blessed were we! The Pelican is mentioned there, the month of the Crab, and all that happened to both of us. Was he visited by Hermes as well? The fisher bird, the Fisher King to whom Parsifal passes the Holy Grail! The three young pelicans must represent the trinity which an ensouled being incarnates. What was to happen next? Would some writing in the Library give me guidance? Adriaan said that I can do the Great Work on my own, if I chose. Opus Magnum was in the area of alchemy and transformation. Would it be the regeneration of the body? What would the consequence be? Do I want to live another hundred years or more? This must be in the later part of my script. Right then I was thrilled about the flow of my comedy and some immortality was not to spoil my excitement.

The weekend was here and I had to give myself time to rest. I decided to become a tourist for two days, visit the Van Gogh museum and the neighbouring one with Rembrandt's works, and cruise on A'dam's canals for a few hours. Even though it was raining, I enjoyed the day very much.

That Sunday night I read the explanation on the symbol of a pelican again. According to it, I had all the tools to start the Great Work by myself. Actually, it was expected of me.

Dante with Beatrice in Paradise, surrounded by John, James and Peter, by William Blake.

Toledo

On Monday morning everyone was in a very cheerful mood at the library. What two days of rest can do to a hard working person! While I was talking to the director regarding a person I was hoping to find in the library, he said that I was the only visitor who was guided to them by the pelican and he felt that I had a genuine guidance. When I was describing my beloved to him and said 'taller than you', he heard 'Toledo' instead. My accent gave me away many times in my life, so I laughed and corrected his misunderstanding. At that very moment the curator was standing next to me, holding a newspaper clip and said, "It is Toledo! Look!" and she showed me the article.

I immediately lit up. "Thank God! You both are messengers!"

They smiled and said that there were no coincidences.

The article was about a Dutch curator who was doing a translation of some old scriptures in Toledo. His last name was Keller. A very similar name to mine. Obviously, Toledo was my next destination. The phone call I received from Spain some twenty months ago still boggled my mind. I felt that Spain had some answers for me and so I decided to travel there on the day after the fourth anniversary.

In the evening I called Nico and Jacob to tell them that I'd visit with them on the way from Spain. My Eurorail ticket could take me anywhere. I just had to pay an extra fee for the couchette.

I phoned the gnostic group in Madrid, to which I sent a letter from Canada. Juan supplied me with addresses of Spanish and Dutch groups, just in case I wanted to get together with them.

Alberto was the person assigned to be my guide once I arrived to Madrid. He had a very pleasant voice and sounded so different from the Chilean Alberto who accompanied me to Mendoza. The following day I went to buy a ticket and to reserve the bed from Paris to Madrid. Everything was set. I had yet plenty of time to study and prepare for the day of the anniversary.

On the day of July 13, 1992, I was full of expectations. Generally, very few people were coming to the library, since it was private and shared by the word of mouths. The staff and volunteers kept very busy with transcriptions and translations. Many visitors would slow down their work.

I was immersed in reading Corpus Hermeticum, and comparing the text with gnostic teachings and opening my mind to this higher philosophy. There were texts on alchemy and healing. There was another earnest student who took notes, just like I did. He was a gentleman in his sixties. At the end of the day, when I went to place the books into their appropriate section, I had to pass by him. He smiled. I could feel a peaceful breeze from him, a very nice energy. He was reading Paracelsus. He left while I was talking to the curator about my trip to Spain. She wished me a wonderful trip hoping that I'd find more answers.

Then I walked toward the door. The older gentleman was waiting there. I thought he was reading something interesting by the entrance. When I picked up my umbrella from the rack, he asked me if he could walk with me to the train station. When I asked him why, he replied that he would like to speak with me.

We stepped out and I covered both of us with my hot pink umbrella, which gave us a healthy glow. He kept on looking into my eyes and smiling.

"What brought you to this library?" he asked.

"A guidance. I just had to come. I had to be here today."

"Why today?"

"It's a long story. I was to meet someone here. A messenger, I guess."

"People come here for all kinds of reasons. I come here to learn about natural healing. I am writing an article on Paracelsus, so I came to do some research."

"Are you a writer?" I asked.

"No, I am a naturopath, but I do some writing in some health magazines. What is your line of work?"

"Right now, I am a massage therapist, but want to study naturopathy in the future."

"I think you should. You have nice energy. Could we keep in touch? I'll give you my address in Amsterdam. Will you write me?"

"Yes, I will write you."

He wrote his name and address for me. He emphasized the meaning of his surname. When I broke his name down it said HER MAN THE DUKE.

"Now, can I walk you to the station?"

"But, I am not going to the station, Herman!"

"I thought you were going to Spain," he answered.

"Have you been listening to my conversation inside the library?"

"I wanted to talk to you, so I waited and overheard your conversation."

"I'll see you on my return from Spain. I should be back on the 2lst. It is the day of my departure. Do you want to meet me here around eleven in the morning, Herman?"

He was very happy about my proposition and agreed to meet me. Then he gave me a little good -bye kiss, wishing me a magical trip.

The train from Brussels to Paris was delayed upon its arrival. I only had 35 minutes to get myself from the Gare du Nord to the Austerlitz station. The Metro connections were poor. I had to take the last section by taxi. I just boarded the train and it began to move. I would've never got my money back if I missed it. We were arriving at Madrid in the morning. I had a good Toledo connection. The ride was about two hours long, but not as interesting. Toledo was the highlight. The train station in Toledo is very ancient, built in a gothic style. It looks more like a chapel.

The bus took me to the center of the city. I found a hotel that accepted VISA and since it was still in renovation, the price was very reasonable. It was named Carlos V., after the inquisitor king. My room number was 207.

Almost immediately I looked up Dr. Keller's name in the phone book. He lived on a nearby street. I walked over. The windows of his apartment were covered by geraniums. The good Dutchman had his garden. He wasn't home. Another tenant, who lived in the complex, gave me his number in Madrid, where he worked on weekdays.

I reached him by phone. I told him that I heard about his work from the people in the Hermetic Library and he told me that he did some work there in the past and named me the people he knew. I knew them too. I told him that I would like to meet with him and discuss something that might interest him. He was coming to Toledo for the weekend and promised to pick me up in the hotel.

I also phoned Alberto. He was to wait for me in Madrid's station on Saturday afternoon.

The rest of Friday I walked through the tiny streets of Toledo, browsing through many stores selling artifacts of gifted local goldsmiths. It is a very peaceful place, built on a fortress, uniting Spanish, Moorish and Jewish cultures. Toledo has a rich past. Not all of it was good. The Inquisition Council had its headquarters there and many bloody tortures had been performed right there. Interesting, how a doctrine of the Catholic Church hoped to spread all over the world by force and by creating fear. The best of the crop, including the most advanced minds of that time, such as inventors, thinkers, and Cathars, were all being prosecuted and eliminated in the cruelest of ways. Toledo's enormous cathedral still emanated horror and shame. I felt much better on the streets among pedestrians, tourists, and merchants at any time of day and night.

Dr. Keller met me in the lobby, as he promised. He was tall, handsome, friendly. We went for a refreshment to the main square's outdoor restaurant and had a good conversation. He couldn't presently recall anyone who resembled the one I was looking for, but wanted to keep a line of communication open. I gave Dr. Keller my Canadian address.

In the afternoon I went by train to Madrid. Alberto was waiting. He was very charming and I trusted him from the very beginning. I had an intention of going to the Prado museum, but had only one hour left. We went to the botanical gardens instead. Alberto was different than most men his age. He was twenty one years younger than me, yet had the maturity of forty year old. He was a musician and loved J. S. Bach the most. He understood his spiritual and musical genius. Alberto was aware of Bach's passion for numerology and its application in his compositions. Besides, Alberto was an artist, specializing in aerography and did many impressive designs. He was very dedicated to gnostic teaching and practiced what he knew in his own life. Because of his maturity he had difficulty relating to women his age. I cherished the time we spent together and regretted that our day was over. In order to stay in Madrid upto Sunday, I needed to find a decent and reasonable place. Nothing was available. I chose to go back to Toledo, since my night was reserved there anyway. Alberto decided to join me. His mother was from Toledo and he loved the city as well. We needed more time together, to get to know each other better. We enjoyed each other's company and shared many ideas.

Alberto was staying in room 306 of the same hotel. He pointed out to me that both our rooms had number 9. We walked and talked until we got hungry. I loved the gazpacho soup. It is so refreshing in summer.

Finally, I asked Alberto a question that waited to be popped out at any moment. He knew someone who matched the description I gave him. He said that his name was Ariel. When I asked him whether or not Ariel travels to Chile, he said that he travels to Argentina to Cordova, where his family was from. Ariel was about 44 years old.

"Where is Ariel now?"

"In Madrid. You can meet him tomorrow. Our group goes to the mountains. You're invited. Some know that you're coming and they would like to meet you."

"Alberto, I don't have hiking boots with me. Tell me more about Ariel. What is his profession?"

"He is a waiter!"

"A waiter? Why?"

"His family owns hotels. He is making sure that all goes well. He is also a devoted Gnostic. He actually introduced me to the movement in 1988. He was my instructor and a friend. He still is."

For the first time during my search I found a matching description, a name that could well be Yariek, but the surname didn't match. I could meet this person the following day and yet, I felt that he wasn't him. I stopped asking about Ariel and showed more interest in Alberto and his inner beauty which reflected on the outside as well. I offered him a massage and he gladly accepted It was more my treat than his. He was fully relaxed and took in what there was available for him. My hands sculpted his young body, making it more beautiful. My hands still hold the memory of his form. He awarded me generously. The next day he gave me one of his paintings. It portrays our solar system within the Milky Way. There was his signature: Alberto Blázquez.

I decided not to go to the mountains. Alberto stayed with me until my train to Barcelona was coming. The last hour our communication was more in feeling than speaking. We both liked each other. I wished we could have a more compatible age. At all times I was watchful so that no spark of intimacy would be ignited. It would be so easy to love him and create a long term relationship.

There was potential. We shared peace and harmony and philosophical belief that not many people are open to. What a dear soul I had to leave behind.

In the last week of preparations for the Olympic Games, Barcelona was the best place to travel to. The police force was everywhere, the city was spotless and people were extremely friendly. I have very fond memories of that Catalan city.

The Winter Olympic Games in Calgary, in 1988 made the city a better place and since then its friendliness grew. Each time people of various backgrounds gather for some kind of higher purpose, it uplifts them and helps the mass consciousness to reach a higher level.

From Alberto to Alberta

I took a night train from Barcelona to Paris and from there another one to Belgium. I had about 20 hours left to spend in Antwerp. Nico was in England and Jan was on vacation. Jacob was available. He was sad that we had very little time together, but was happy about the progress I was making in my search and invited me to Brecht. This time we didn't go for beer, but went for coffee and pastries. He was putting on some weight and I believed that his diet had something to do with it. He promised that the next time I'll see him he'd be thinner.

We still had the same good rapport. That likely will never change. He was sceptic about the Dante and Beatrice incarnations. Intuitively, he was accepting the reincarnation concept, but his carnal mind fashioned by catholicism opposed his feelings. I let it rest and spoke about a different subject. I just told him that the pelican in the library's emblem represented Hermes. Jacob wasn't interested to hear about Hermes. He felt it was connected to practices of magic and he feared it.

I stayed overnight at his Mom's house. His father had passed away during the past year.

The next morning I was on my way to Amsterdam, and to Canada. I fell asleep on the train and mistakenly got off in Rotterdam. The next train to Amsterdam was a slow detour train, so I arrived to the Library for the afternoon. I had to leave in less than two hours. The secretary had two messages for me. One was from Herman, who waited for me upto noon. He had patients for the afternoon. He couldn't come back. The next message was from a to me unknown person, who actually called the library before my departure for Spain. He wanted to talk to me. I called him.

He spoke very nice English and had a lovely and trustworthy tone of voice. He was from Rotterdam. I told him that I was leaving for Canada and must be at the Schiphol airport by five the latest to check my luggage in. He said he would wait for me at quarter to five at the meeting place. When I asked him how I would recognize him, he said to me not to worry, that he would recognize me. I liked this mystery man. Who ever he was, he was in my script. I didn't feel at all that he would be my beloved. I felt he was a very important messenger.

After making a few more photocopies of writings and sharing a bit of my Spain adventure with the curator, I was on my way to the airport. I was curious about my new messenger and truly wondered how anyone who hadn't seen me yet could recognize me.

I was approaching the famous meeting place full of people. Surely enough, a tall man in his late thirties was walking toward me. He had dark hair and glasses."Are you Ms. Heller from Canada?"

"Yes, I am. How do you know about me?"

He showed me a letter I sent to Rotterdam's Gnostic group. He was their instructor. Now I was clear on the mystery. His name was Juan too. He figured that I didn't have enough time to visit with their group, so he decided to meet me personally. Every Gnostic is a special person, he said.

"How do you tell a Gnostic?" I asked.

"I could pick you in the crowd, Ingrid!"

"But I am not a Gnostic," I corrected him.

"You are not? What are you, then? What are you seeking?"

"I cannot label myself. I don't want to label myself. I am seeking the Knowledge of the Heart, the Truth."

"That is Gnosis, Ingrid." Juan answered with calm confidence.

My turn in the line was coming. We were already announced that our charter flight was delayed four hours. I checked my luggage in and Juan invited me for a beer. A good conversation was destined to follow.

Juan asked me what I was doing in the Library and how I found out about it. I told him that a few years ago I saw the emblem and later on found out that it belonged to the library. I also told him about the gnostic video Juan in Calgary loaned me.

Juan looks at me as if he knew I wasn't tellimg him the whole story. "Ingrid, you are looking for someone, are you not?"

"Yes, for someone I'd already met four years ago in Santiago de Chile. I truly believed that I'll find him in Europe."

"You will find him when you least expect it. It can happen in your own living room."

"If it would be that easy, why am I making this trip, seeking?"

"It is the search of yourself within yourself, Ingrid. You probably look too much for him outside yourself....Is he your beloved twin?"

My eyes must had answered it all.

"Do you truly love him, Ingrid?"

"What a question! Of course I love him. I love him the most of all people on Earth."

"Then release him. Let him go!"

"Juan, that is too much to ask of me. I cannot let him go. He is with me, always on my mind!"

"Do you want to find him?"

"Of course, I do! That's why I am here, Juan!"

"Exactly! You have to transform it by letting him go and stop looking for him."

I began to cry. Juan touched my hand and very kindly continued his message. "Ingrid, by letting go and releasing you step to a higher level. Each time you want to transform something you have to clear everything, let go of everything. He is on a higher level waiting for you. He is not on this one anymore. That happened in Santiago. Go upward. Climb the mountain! If you just knew how blessed you are!"

I was still sobbing. "Juan, how can I possibly release him? How can I do it?"

"Love someone else!"

"I cannot love anyone else. He is my ultimate love!"

"You said it: the ultimate. You can have other relationships before him. Try! It is worth trying. You are loving, attractive, you will be able to create a relationship with someone else. You will see!"

"I've met some lovely men on this trip. One of them is Gnostic and knows about sacred matrimony."

"Perfect! Start right there. The magic will happen."

I observed Juan while he was talking to me. He had the same light in his eyes I noticed in the other Juan and in Alberto. All of them worked constructively with their sexual energy. They didn't waste. They used it for their own regeneration.

"Ingrid, what if your twin is married?"

"I doubt it. He had no ring."

"In some cultures men do not wear one. What if he is married?"

I didn't feel very comfortable about it. On the other hand, I was relieved. It actually felt liberating that my twin would have someone to love him, to cook for him, care for him, and hopefully be the mother of his children. I knew that my beloved lived in denial in the past lives and needed the balance that a married life sometimes brings.

Juan inspected my eyes, noticing that I was thinking about this possibility. "Ingrid, you did not answer me yet! Would you pursue if he was married?"

"No. I would wait until he is free. I would love to be his and his wife's friend, though."

"Good. You are ready then."

We paused for a while. I wondered whether Juan's questions were suggestions, tests, or messages. Then I asked him about his path and gnosticism. We ended up talking about alchemy and alchemical marriage. I was actually a married woman. I was fully committed to my beloved and to my soul's guidance.

Juan had to go back to Rotterdam. He was teaching a class that night. Later on I received a lovely card from him with words of encouragement and friendship, and an instruction: teach your beloved the path of sacred matrimony.

The charter flight was delayed another three hours. I arrived to Calgary in the early morning. Eduardo was kind to pick me up and to take me to my children, who were waiting for me since the last night.

I thought a lot of Juan's words and sincerely tried to follow on his instruction. I could not live with an empty heart. As far as I remembered, I always loved someone. If it wouldn't be my cousin, it would be my teacher, then some movie star, my brother's classmates, and toward my 16 years of age I began to date a real people. My heart was always loving. In my troubled marriages the love was focused on my children. All I knew was love. There was no way that I would empty my heart in order to transform the present situation. I had to replace my beloved.

On the day of my arrival I phoned Alberto. He was ecstatic that I called him. He said that he missed me and asked how I felt about both of us. I told him the truth that I cared about him and felt lots of love for him. He cried in joy and exclaimed couple times "I knew you would love me, I just knew it!"

I wrote Alberto a letter on the same day. I had to be realistic. The age difference was scary. Many people on the Path claim that age doesn't matter. It did with me. I had children, I had to set an example and Monica's boyfriend was of Alberto's age. My letter didn't come out all so negative. There was a bond we'd created in Spain. It was a much older connection without identification of any incarnation we might have shared. There was the unity that all people will eventually reach when they learn about unconditional love and the respect for each other. The oneness some idealistic philosophies talk about. I felt a very strong love for my artistic friend whose spirituality reflected in his work and in his countenance.

A r i e l

The following day I received a phone call from the lady naturopath. She asked me when I'd be able to start at her clinic. I explained my situation to her. I had no car, no money to buy one, and my home was far from her clinic. It would take me at least two hours by bus each way to get to her clinic. She was generous and offered that if I work with her, she'd co-sign a loan for a car. Eduardo loaned me his old car in the meanwhile. He used another one. I was mobile and able to start to work.

I liked the work and soon got used to the international clientele she had. I was becoming very involved with my training and that way kept my mind off relationships. I was focused on my future profession and on my children. Ray's condition was stable, which contributed to my peace. I was also doing internal cleansing with colonic irrigations and followed a diet rich in minerals, and soon I began to feel more energetic than before. I did a regular exercise and slept on my massage table. All was going smoothly and well.

Two weeks later I had a very vivid dream where Alberto ran toward me exclaiming in Spanish: "Ingrid, Ingrid, it is Ariel, it is Ariel! He remembers you from Santiago! He remembers you from Santiago!" With it came a very loving energy. Alberto was holding my right hand when he was passing me the second half of the message. I felt filled with ardent love again. The flame that was slowly dying in me was growing bigger. I wrote Ariel a letter the next morning, sending it to the Gnostic group in Madrid. Maybe it was him and I was not ready to meet him again while in Spain. I remembered that Aaron once told me that it makes no difference where I look for him that, eventually, he'll pop out of my interior and I'll meet him in my own living room. Juan said the same thing.

Was Ariel coming back because I released him? Was Alberto's role to enchant me with his inner and outer beauty so I could make this important step? Would my bodily cleansing change my frequency and help me to get to the next level? Whatever it was, I was filled with life again. Clients noticed my radiance and I credited it to the cleanse. Everybody wanted to do theirs. I was their inspiration!

The week passed. Hanna came back from her vacation. She was overwhelmed about my story and insisted I must write a book about my journey. I received letters from Jacob, Herman, and none yet from Alberto. His painting decorated a wall in my massage room, where I slept. Him and Salvador Dali were my favourite Spanish painters. I was fond of art. My walls were covered by copies of masterpieces, some special originals and a series of Art Nouveau by Alfonse Mucha. I loved my home full of music, artwork, books, and children.

On Friday night I waited for midnight to phone Alberto. I didn't want to wake him up too early. I was a sweet awakening for him. He already received my letter and was to write me back. We talked about us and a possible conflict due to our age difference. Alberto still believed that it should create no problem, but I could feel that he wasn't so sure anymore. Then I asked him about his friend Ariel. He was presently in Argentina. I asked Alberto if he possibly knew where Ariel was in July of '88 and he answered with certainty that he was in Madrid.

"But how can you know, Alberto? It's been four years!"

"Ingrid, exactly at that time I was joining the Gnostic Movement and Ariel was my number one teacher. We worked together in the hotel at that time. I know he was in Madrid!"

There was very little left for me to say. I was disappointed with my dream. Dreams used to be such a faithful friend to me and now they were misguiding me. I had to release all: Ariel, Alberto and any potential partner. It was a week of death. My heart was aching. There was a void.

The lady naturopath noticed that something was missing. The next Thursday she asked me why I didn't date anyone. I told her that the one I would love to be with I haven't found yet. She said that she will find me a good Jewish man. She was Jewish, I wasn't. I told her that my man is someone very special and that I chose to wait for him and noone else, but presently, I had many other things to do in life and a relationship wasn't a priority.

The Friday night I received a phone call from my friend Val. She is a very caring soul and was concerned about my education. She offered money for my pathology class, so I could continue with studies. I told her about the dream I had and how it turned out. She knew about my quest and assured me that something special would happen soon. Then she suggested to date someone anyway.

"No, Val. I am not ready for anyone else. I'll transform that love to my friends, patients. I love people anyway. It is not going to be that difficult. My work leads me in that direction. I'll be fine, Val. I don't feel lonely. I work with people, have four children at home and am very fortunate to have friends like yourself."

She wished me good luck for the auditions we had on Saturday. Music filled me again. In the morning I practiced several of Bach's pieces at the piano and added my Ombra Mai Fu. This time I sang it to the world. My voice was ready.

At the audition I sang Suscepit Israel and some randomly selected pieces from other cantatas. I was invited to come back to our rehearsals. There were some new lovely voices. Our new conductor was an accomplished pianist and had very lovely energy.

Andrew and Maria went with Eduardo for the weekend and I was left with Jean and Joe. We watched the review of a series of the English comedy The Faulty Towers. Did we ever laugh! I needed humour and laughter. It was healing. It was a marvelous day.

On Sunday I was left alone in the house, having plenty of time to myself. For the first time in my life I didn't feel like doing anything. I had no desire to listen to music or to sing, neither to get to my chores. I was sitting on the sofa in the living room, feeling an absolute emptiness.

A sudden impulse led me to the sound system and I turned on the radio. A very sweet energy poured over me at that moment and I rushed to see myself in the mirror to witness the Soul presence within my body. I was glowing! I heard an introduction to the "Writer's Company" and to the guest writer, poet, and play-wright Ariel Dorfman, born in Argentina, a Chilean citizen, who was a visiting professor at the Duke University. I heard my Ariel's voice! It was the voice I heard on inner levels! The interview was dynamic. How can anyone answer the way I would had answered? And his manner of speech was similar to mine! He recited poems from his collection The Last Waltz in Santiago. The poem Vocabulary mentioned our encounter. I finally got an idea to tape his voice. Other books and his successful play Death and the Maiden were mentioned. I wasn't myself. I was half stiff and cold, touched by a magic wand. I wanted to drop to my knees and thank God for his guidance. I wanted to shout in joy, compose my first symphony, write another poem. I wanted to make this day of August 29th of 1992 memorable to the world. Ariel! What a beautiful name his parents had given him!

I phoned Hanna immediately after the program. She was excited and exclaimed, "The best news in years! This is him!"

I played her the tape through the phone receiver. She was even more positive about him.

"It is your voice in a masculine version, Ingrid! It is like listening to you! Oh, this is exciting!"

Hanna was truly happy for me. When Jean and Joe returned from their Dad's place in the evening, I asked Jean to borrow Ariel's books in the library for me. On Friday she brought me The Last Waltz in Santiago and reserved The Hard Rain, My House Is On Fire, Mascara, and The Last Song of Manuel Sendero.

I looked at the book's jacket and held before me an image that enchanted me four years earlier. Poems like Habeas Corpus and Something More than Lightbulbs tore my heart. Then I read Occupation Army: "On this street corner in Santiago, Huérfanos and Ahumada ......Each time you pass by, like a broken record that someone tries to play just one more time...... In Santiago you go past that corner. I cannot."

He's been looking for me through his poetry, while I've been seeking places, asking the guardians at the gates about my consort King. Now I had to find the way to his Kingdom. Does the man of exile have his Kingdom?

My comedy reached its highest point. My dreams and guidances had never failed me! How could I ever doubt? The messengers came my way! I was the author, actor, and director again. My Dante came back! The A and D woven into the towels my mother sent me! ARIEL, the name given to the winged LION of God.

P a m e l a

There are stories that are sacred and must be kept secret. The profane should never know about them. How could they possibly understand, being so far from the Truth? Some stories are sacred, but must be told. The seekers on the Path to completion need an inspiration.

I was holding The Last Song of Manuel Sendero, that claimed to be the best seller. There were chapters on Incarnation and many Outside and Inside stories, and much more. I was anxious and read through the pages. The story of David had to be told. The story of Manuel and his love for his twin Pamela intervenes with David's. I reached page 34 and read about the encounter of the two souls who broke the rebelion of the unborn against the incarnation, and chose to be born to change the world. Pamela went to experience her life in Chile first. Prior to her incarnation she agreed to meet Manuel in the downtown of Santiago, where he located her in the crowd nearby the demonstrators. He tried to tell her that he knew her for a very long time, since they were very small. At first, Pamela didn't believe him but when she experienced telepathy with him, she understood and believed.

The book was written in 1982, when Ariel was in exile, living in Washington D.C. and I was living in Chile, working the land, giving birth to my brave Maria, who came to this world in a lotus position. I came in first and it was my responsibility to meet him. Six years prior to our encounter he wrote about us. Hence comes the name Pamela.

The man who knows his script, the director, narrator, the actor committed to his comedy. From the Exile he returned to Eden to experience Paradise because he had already eaten of the Fruit of Knowledge of Good and Evil, completing with the cycle, according to the Law. Being no more washed by the Waters of Lethe, preserving the memory of the Past, Present and Future. The unfinished had to be completed on a personal level, relationships with all kingdoms of nature and the service on the levels that are reserved for the Kings. The voice of Manuel Sendero, his song and word, the Logos.

All my dreams, guidances, and messages came back to me in a flash. All were genuine and true. Did I really have to wait for four years to find out? What would happen if the story continued the way it is in Ariel's book on the following pages? Would the attraction satisfy the longing of the inner doves? In divine comedies there are no earthly duties. The magic flute would play her tune and the test of fire and water would have to be passed.

Truly, I could not imagine my possible behaviour, if we began to talk on that street location. I would likely do something unusual, totally original, out of this world. Would that be a line in my comedy? What had taken place in my script was correct. Ariel calls his novel a fiction, I call mine a true story. A fiction writer is frequently ahead of his time. He can be a genius, inventor, or a prophet.

I was compelled to call the Duke University. I called and had succeeded in having a good conversation with Ariel's secretary. I left the message and began to prepare a tape with spoken letter. I was ready for the unexpected.

All my friends were an encouraging influence and some could not understand why I didn't travel to Durham. My reply was simple: my comedy was developing so nicely, I was not going to rush it and have it over with. There is time and space for everything and my interior was to reveal the right time to me. I had professional plans, I had to become financially independent and much wiser. I had no rush. Besides, Ariel had two sons and a wife who stood by him through the harrowing times of the exile years. She was his woman. I was not. She gave him children and freed me of that responsibility. The Sarah story was not my case anymore.

I mailed the tape and had all the time in the world for the answer. The ultimate, the best is for the last. My task was to fill in the lines between, speak them clearly, live them fully.

I thought I had everything under control. I found my man. What then? Was I supposed to wait for him for the rest of my life? Could I have other relationships before him? What was going on in Ariel's head? Was he going to write, visit, phone? Was I to wait for his next book to figure out what was happening? At times I wasn't as patient. There were days when I sat next to the telephone hoping that the next call would be from Ariel. Marc bought me a phone with an answering system so I could have my peace while being away from home.

I worked only part-time at that time. The children didn't have to be driven to schools anymore. Joe and Jean took a bus to their high school and Maria and Andrew walked to the recently constructed school in our neighbourhood. My Pathology class was at night. I had a new car that looked much better than any other I had owned before.

Hanna and my other good friends were all waiting for my call from Ariel. Val and Sue gave me The Last Waltz in Santiago for my birthday. Ray phoned to wish me a Happy Birthday and asked how things were. I told him about the radio interview and the books. His reaction shocked me. He literally said to me that he lost all respect for me because I believed that some interviewed writer was my beloved. I recited the poem about our encounter. He got even more furious. Then he asked whether the author sent me a bouquet of flowers for my birthday or phoned me from the airport. I realized that I couldn't share my joy with Ray. He was on a different plane of consciousness, fighting for his life.

The days were adding up. I began to doubt that Ariel got any message from me, nor received my cassette letter. I turned to the pages of his books and received comfort there. Manuel loved Pamela! In the book Mascara, Oriana became an obsession for the narrator. She was so different from the rest of the world that she had to be protected. Pages and pages were speaking to me. The masques that introduced themselves to me on the night of June 21st of 1989 indicated the title of this book!

When I was about to finish the course, I took on another job. I was hired as a masseuse in a chiropractor's office and had to look for my own clientele to earn money. It worked out pretty well. I worked seven days a week. Not all hours were filled with work. On Saturdays I was back with waitressing. I had to fill my time to make waiting easier. I wondered how many more hours, days, or weeks I had to wait.

I phoned Ariel's secretary again. She said that the tape was passed to him when it arrived Why wasn't I hearing from him? His secretary claimed that he was an extremely busy man. How much time does a short note take? Something was happening that I didn't understand. There is no script without communication. One of my lines was missing. I had to create a change that would trigger progress, give me some incentive, inspire me to the next step. I hoped that the upcoming Christmas would bring the newness and help me to transform the present situation.

I wrapped a special gift for Ariel and placed it under our Christmas tree. It was a custom made pendant made of Chilean copper that I wore at the time of our encounter. It had the shape of a leaf, with my name engraved on it . It was given to me by Eduardo's sister many years ago. The heart shaped leaf was a symbol of a leaf from our Tree of Life. Copper is the metal of Venus, the Goddess of Love. The pendant was made to be given to my love to wear.

I sent off all Christmas mail and chose a special card for Ariel, hoping that the card and the words would create a response. Yet, I was peaceful and patient. Time didn't matter. Time is linear. The quality of time mattered. I quit my waitressing job and stayed with my profession only. I had Christmas holidays reserved for my family and friends. My heart was celebrating the union of Adam and Eve. I sang the sacred music daily. I sang in celebration of Melchizedek's son.

E d e n

The winter was tough. As a matter of fact, there were days when our cars froze up and we had to wait for minus twenty degrees to defrost it. On those days I had to skip work. It didn't harm anyone - clients would cancel anyway. I had time to plan and study.

Ray was in and out of the hospital. He was on oxygen all the time. He was thin and had little energy left. Information came my way about Hydrazine Sulfate that would stop the cancer growth, but I couldn't obtain it anywhere. Antineoplastons were costly and he would have to travel to obtain them. I heard about the success of Russian physicians with their research on urine therapy. Terminal cancer patients were recovering. Ray felt a bit reluctant about drinking the 'Elixir of Life'. He still believed in a miracle cure and hoped to have more time granted to make some spiritual breakthrough.

In my colon therapy course ozone therapy was mentioned along with its beneficial effects in the treatment of cancer and many other diseases. I had to do something quickly to keep Ray among the living a bit longer. The impulse came very powerfully: I was to start my own clinic of alternative therapies. The health care system was in debt and we had to help to reduce it by taking good care of ourselves. I knew that a right moment would indicate itself to find a clinic location and get started. At this point I had no money to start with, but my credit cards represented some. I was preparing, studying, practicing. All clients I had at this time would follow me and they would refer their friends. I ordered the best massage table on the market and at the end of February I felt strongly that a certain location in the northwest of Calgary was available for me. I drove through. I found one place, but the realtor had a more affordable one coming up soon. He gave me the address. It was a place I always liked for its exposure to the public and traffic. For years, as I had been driving by, I said to myself that one day, when I'd have my own business, I would like to lease a space in that building. Now, it was available to me.

All dealings with the realtor and the landlord went well. I still didn't have the money I needed for numerous deposits. I committed myself to March 8th. The realtor asked why March 8th. I told him that it was a day when I'd have the money. He knew that I was a single mother and he felt that my resources were limited. On March 7th I had the money and phoned him. When he came with the offer contract he asked me about my magic. I told him about my three lady friends who loaned me eight thousand among themselves.

"But how could you be so sure about the day?" he asked.

"It is in my destiny, I am to have that clinic. That is why all flows."

"Teach me, show me your magic!" he said.

"You already found it. You trusted."

He turned out to be a good supportive client, and every time he came we had a good talk and much more laughter.

The clinic location was to be available for May 1st 1993. I had a perfect place for every object, picture, poster, and plant. It was to be a healing place with a subtle message to everyone who walked in. The fig tree Ray gave me a long time ago was to be the major point of attraction by the entrance. The Tree of Life at Eden. I had the name for the clinic: Eden Wholistic Clinic. And I had the snake for the tree! I had the location, the well put together brochure, and the business cards.

Excited about the project, I rushed to share the news with Ray. He was still hanging on. On March 31st I went to see him in the hospital. It was right before Easter and I knew that the Easter lilies I brought would make him happy. He acknowledged them, but could not smell them. He couldn't swallow anything either. I told him about ozone therapy and that he would be my first ozone client. He just said that he was very happy for me and my clinic and that he knew that I'd do lots of good. I described the place to him and how beautiful the Tree of Life from him would look there and that it would always remind me of him. He showed a little spark in his eyes, which had no colour left in them. He asked me if I could move his legs to another position. They were thin, but extremely heavy. His spirit was leaving. I told him that I'd come back tomorrow and would bring his favourite poetry. He told me not to worry about tomorrow. At that moment I knew that he was leaving us. I sat next to him on the bed, embraced him and then I took his head, holding it against my heart, rocking him gently, making a connection. It was the only connection his head and mind had ever made to any heart. I kissed his crown and gently placed his head on the pillow, softly saying "See you tomorrow, Ray... ."

On the way home I cried. I looked back at his life and I ached. How many other people have their dreams that never come true? How many people are there who do something else than they were born for, never find their purpose in life, never read their own comedy. Why? Because they are afraid of change, of the unknown, living by earthly duty and never daring to make a move. Each of them becoming a copy of each other. How can the world progress with repeated history and do-alikes? How can we possibly return to Eden with the attitude of masses? There was no way I would succumb to that movement. I was to go ahead, trusting, feeling the guidance of the spirit. Fools Day was coming and the Fool in Tarot has the highest value. It is Zero, representing the new beginning with infinite possibilities, the continuance. A circle is the symbol for the universe without the beginning and without the end. Just like the snake biting on its own tail is representing the same.

The next day was extremely foggy and I chose not to drive to the hospital. I phoned instead. They didn't have Ray on the list. Another nurse was passed to me. She asked what my relation was with Mr. Knight. I told her that I was just a friend. She found my name on the file.

"Ms. Heller, Mr. Knight passed away last night."

I was silent for a while. I was not surprised. I believed he went through the transition shortly after I left. The nurse gave me the public trustees' phone number.

Ray didn't make it to April Fool's Day. Perhaps, he died on Fool's Day and the next time around he'll choose a white dog to guide him through life, the way it was on the Celtic deck of Tarot cards he gave me.

The public trustee had no name of his relatives. I gave him some information. No one else called about Ray. The funeral service was announced in the newspaper. When I was coming to the funeral home, there was no other car parked. I asked if it was the right hour and the right place. It was. Ray's corpse looked peaceful. I placed one red rose into his hands and two red roses I crossed over his chest vertically and horizontally. The knight, the crusador, had his symbol. Without love and a lady to fight for he lost his sword.

Two other people came to his funeral service. One was a nurse who said that he was such a gentleman and a sweet man. The other one was his aging neighbour, who sometimes talked with him in the laundry area of the apartment building of eighteen floors. I followed Ray's body upto the burrial grounds and made sure that the red roses were put to rest with him.

It was the saddest funeral I had ever went to. It wasn't my baby Jane's, who coincidently passed away on the same day nineteen years earlier, neither my father's. Ray was lonely and he died lonely and that should never happen to anyone. He was a gentleman with the name that was trying to tell him about his mission. He just never paid attention to it.

There are many mansions in the kingdom, many pathways. We each follow just one. Mine was to lead me to Eden, to learn about the Tree of Life. I placed the tree of life into my clinic's logo, and encoded the chemical symbol for ozone into it. My quest became the fruit of the tree from the middle of the garden.

L a m e n

The first month at the clinic was very busy and it kept on getting busier all the time. Clients were coming back and many were attracted to the regeneration program I was offering. Each and every client became my partner teacher and student, everyone was so different from the other, so special. My days were long. I worked near ninety hours a week. I had no day off, but I loved my work and my clients. The place was bright with daylight and the plants were in their seasonal bloom, sharing the gift of fragrance. Emotionally and mentally I danced, going with the rhythm, harmony, and the flow.

Jean helped a bit at home and watched over Maria and Andrew during the summer vacation. We had no more financial stress, but I had very little time for my children. It made me feel guilty. When I got home after work, I did the clinic's laundry, cooking, research work for my clients, and touched the base with the children, if they were still awake. As busy as I was, I began to miss Ariel again. Why didn't he write or phone? I phoned his editor and she asked me to send a letter for him through her, promising that she'd make sure he gets it. I mailed a registered letter in August.

Eden was ready for my Adam. My friend Tamarah hung the red apples on the Tree of Life. Special items in every room were ready to welcome my other half. Where was he? When was he going to appear? Each morning, when I scanned the messages on my answering machine, I hoped I'd hear his voice. .

Labour Day came. It was a warm sunny day and it became my first day off, dedicated to labour - my home was turned into an immaculate place. In the afternoon, when I washed my living room window, a neighbour offered to take my children to the nearby Nose Hill Park. Her son was a sweet child, appreciating playmates. I consented. Within minutes I felt an urge to go to the clinic and check the messages. Then I began to think that I was becoming attached to my clinic and must learn to be away from it for a day, at the least. Any attachment was unhealthy.and created an emotional co-dependency. I fought my desire and won. Still, I felt that my neighbour was actually giving me a message to go to the clinic and take a break. The clinic became my sanctuary where I felt absolutely at peace and at my full power. I finished the window instead, hung the curtains, and went on to the next one. When the children returned, we all took a break and enjoyed our tea time together. Again, the feeling to go to the clinic came back. I was hesitant. Why was this happening to me? Couldn't I be separated from Eden for one day?

In the morning I got the children off to school. It was a nice feeling to have them back in their routine and with many friends. Jean and Joe entered grade twelve. Monica had a job in Swift Current. She wanted to stay there. She was very much in love with a local man.

I rushed to the clinic to be there before ten. I turned on my messages. Obviously, many callers who left no message. One beep after the other. Then my masseuse left a message and, again, many beeps. A male voice came in, leaving the most unusual statement, addressed to me. It was a two line poem and finished with the word LAMEN. It was Ariel's voice! I taped the message and kept on taping it until I had many calls from him between the beeps. Hanna recognized him as well. Sue and Val, the voice experts, also identified it with Ariel's. Finally, he got my letter! The message was so precious that even if I never heard from him again, I would accept it and look forward to the next incarnation. The word Lamen was a new word in my vocabulary. What does it mean? Could it be in Sanscrit, or in Hebrew? I called a friend professor from the department of classics. Lamen was not in his dictionaries. My Jewish friend Iris suggested the word Lamed, which means to learn, or the introspection. What was I to learn that was so important for the next act of my comedy? More I listened to the message, more I was sure that the word was Lamen. No New Age devotee, nor a self proclaimed spiritual leader or a mystical teacher knew the word. Aaron was living in Okanagan Valley with his family. I phoned him, but he wasn't familiar with the word either. Well, I decided to follow Juan's technique and release it. It would appear again at the right time.

New clients were coming in, but no Adam. Actually, none of them was named Adam. Even Romeo walked through the door. One new acquientence passed me a business card with the logo of a bitten apple. He felt we had something in common. We both got a taste of knowledge. He was good in quoting other people, and chose well. At times he made me laugh. He didn't inspire me much, but I learned from him the slogan "The good man is hard to find, but the hard man is good to find".

Aaron dropped by on his visit to Calgary. He liked the clinic and encouraged me to give my Adam a chance.

"He is busy with something right now. Be patient, Ingrid. He is on his way."

"That damn Adam!" I responded. "He takes detours to Eden!"

"You're not angry with him, are you?"

"Yes, I am. All these years I've been waiting, looking for him, and when I finally find him and wait for him at Eden, he keeps silent. He doesn't even have the guts to leave his name on the tape! He leaves me Lamen instead!"

Aaron looked straight at me, smiling.omnisciently. Then he placed both hands over my cheeks and said very lovingly, "All is upto you, Ingrid! You have the power to recognize the ripe fruit, so you can hand it to him. Look, how many people come to you for help, trusting you. You are a teacher! You've created something special, you had the courage. Why?"

I finished the line for him. "Because it is in my destiny and it is in my script. Aaron, if Ariel is not in my destiny for this lifetime, I want to go beyond. I want to pass all possible reincarnations in this lifetime. I don't want to wait forever among the unborn for some fertile couple and look for my beloved again. I want him this time around, before I am wrinkled and weak."

"You, Ingrid? You are regenerating before our eyes, you are looking younger each time! What is your secret?"

"You know what it is. Right around the corner is our initiation room," I said, leading Aaron to the colonic room. "I am the guardian of the threshold at the bottom level!" We both laughed.

Again, I was privileged to receive Aaron's hug. We don't say good-bye. We just silently part, knowing that we'd cross each other's path again.

A few days later my friend Tamarah phoned me all excited that Ariel's play Death and the Maiden is on in Calgary. She bought me a ticket for the first night. I was ecstatic and anxious to see it. Was he so busy with this work that he could not place me into his life at that time?

After the last client left, I browsed through the clinic, feeling at peace. It was a sacred place, vibrant, filled with gorgeous music. I just wished I could show the place to Ariel. I read his creation - his books. I had nothing written for him, I was not an author. I was in healing arts, opening doorways, introducing another face of God with great faith in human being. God with laughter, and the humour. If God didn't have a sense of humour, He would not had created us.

I sat down at the reception desk, scanning the space. The Goethe's words that were posted on the white wall of the hallway had met my sight: "Upon Faith, Love, Hope rests man's God - favored Religion, Art, Science. These nurture and satisfy the desire to revere, to evoke, to behold. All three are one at the beginning and at the end, even if divided in the middle."

Snow began to fall in large flakes. They reflected against the clinic's lit up sign. One by one, grounding themselves to form a white carpet. To the observer they all look the same, but in reality each of them has one identical partner in design, and both are different from others.

I phoned the children. Most of them were already asleep. The heavy wet snow made the roads a bit slippery. I drove home slowly, but had the feeling of being protected. What shall I do tonight to treat myself? Suddenly, it occurred to me that I never read in detail the Canto XXVI of Dante's Divine Comedy. Is there some message for me, an inspiration to the next line? I brought the copy with me from A'dam's library and later on bought Giardi's translation. Why hadn't I looked into it yet?

Canto XXVI

When everyone was in bed and I knew that I would not be disturbed, I reached for my treasured file where I kept copies of The Divine Comedy. The ritual of reading the special material of meditative nature brought about an atmosphere that was sacred, had within itself a sound of silence opening doorways to understanding and attunment with the writer and the author behind and between the lines. I was about to read the words of my beloved, of my Dante, who came back as a master of letters again.

Dante leaves us in the eighth sphere of the fixed stars. Examination of Love – Adam.

The poet is questioned by John about the way he came to the Possession of Love through Beatrice's eyes, that dazzled the poet and he lost his sight. "Because the eyes of the Lady, through this land Divine conducting thee, irradiate the power that was in Ananias' hand."

Dante answered, "Unto these eyes of mine, which were the gate when she brought in the fire that burns undying, come healing at her pleasure, soon or late. The Good, to this high court all satisfying, is Alpha and Omega of the scroll. Love reads me loudly or softly."

Anxiously I took the copy of Giardi's translation from my bookcase, to compare the text. It was almost identical. I continued reading from the book.

Poet: "By the arguments of philosophy and by authority that descends from here such Love has clearly stamped its seal upon me..."

When the poet is describing love as divine, coming from praise of God, his sight is restored.

"So from my eyes, my lady's eyes, whose ray was visible from a thousand miles and more, drove every last impediment away."

Beatrice : "In that ray's Paradise the first soul from the hand of the First Power turns ever to its maker its glad eyes."

Dante meets with Adam and asks him many questions.

At this point I asked myself, "When does the man meet Adam?" I had the answer, "When he has gone full circle of existences, being no more man of Exile, but returning home to Eden, having his Vigil, his Sophia with him. He becomes Antropos, the complete perfected archetypal man. His sight is restored and he becomes as god."

I remembered the lecture from many years ago to which Trevor came, where the speaker spoke of The Nag Hammadí Library. She also spoke of her vision of Antropos, and the frequency of the New Paradise, the Eden to come, without the Tree of Knowledge of Good and Evil, but with the Tree of Life from the middle of the garden. This lady was a healer whose life was an inspiration. She was driven by Divine Love and transformed her life situation with victory, yet, she was so humble. Humility comes from living the truth and from the enlightenment. Pride comes from ignorance.

Ariel emanated the light of Antropos. During those few seconds of our rapture he identified himself to me. He represented my bride-groom, my Adam, my Antropos, my other half, my twin, my beloved. He was my male and pierced my heart with an arrow so the Eros would never die again and the power of love would burn all sins, transform the imperfect each time I was rewinding the scene of our encounter, just like the broken record. As long as I did that, I was running on my own battery, regenerating. The fire of divine love is the key. Indeed, my name was well chosen for me with INRI placed into it.

Ariel gave me the name Oriana in his book Mascara. Or is it just my imagination? How about the pages 80 and 81 of his book? Eighty one was Dante's favourite number. It is the second power of three. I read the second half of page 80, where Ariel speaks of himself being more fortunate than Adam. He wrote, "She is as Eve. But, I shall not be Adam. I shall be God and the Serpent rolled up into one, starting the day as God and ending it as the Serpent, with the chance to begin the next day another story, a new galaxy, another Garden and another Exile, until the end of time. I can rewrite and recapture the whole of human history. We can be each of the past's lovers, each character in each novel: and it will always be my narrating her, a thousand and one times, if that is necessary."

Is there some message for me in his other works? I had to die to become the maiden.

I died on that street corner in Santiago, being the maiden ready for the marriage feast.

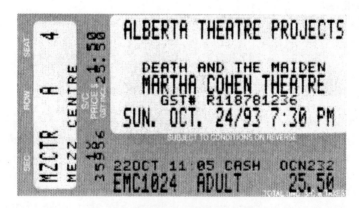

The ticket to the play Death and the Maiden for its first night opening performance.

Death and the Maiden

The 24th of October of 1993 was a special day. I was going to witness the success of Ariel's play. I read the play script just a few months earlier, therefore being aware what the play was all about. It wasn't my favourite theme, but it was an important play. I had a lot in common with my twin, but had a different view on political and social systems. I believed in the evolution of consciousness, and absolutely, in no shortcuts. People earn what they are. They unfold as a blossom, gradually, in seasons of their development. The stem must be strong, or the flower will bend with the first blow of the wind. Whatever happened in some countries is the reflection of their inner state and the consciousness of the general populace. No country can be rushed through changes without preparing its people. The lack of readiness will manifest somewhere, the evident imbalance will be the result.

I closed the clinic a bit earlier to prepare for the date with Ariel's creation. I wore my favourite emerald green suit, with matching jewellery. The theatre was full. I looked into the program and started to read the interview with the playwright, but could not finish. The director introduced the first opening night and, the show began.

We saw the interior of the beachhouse where Pauline is setting a candle light dinner, waiting for her husband. She plays the music Ombra Mai Fu, sang by a gorgeous mezzosoprano voice. It cut through me. It couldn't be a coincidence that the piece I sang for my beloved almost daily was placed in his play! How many more surprises was I to experience? I identified Schubert's Death and the Maiden with the motif of Death from Tristan and Isolde by Richard Wagner. Both pieces create a pull on our soul, like drawing us toward death without our resistance, opening for us a doorway to the magical transition. The play finished with the concert to which all three characters went to hear the Schubert's motif again, to heal, to forgive, to begin a new life. A well done play.

During the intermission I could overhear people talking about the play and Ariel's other works. I went to the play alone for many reasons. I wanted to feel rather than speak. The heart was my feeling brain. At home I finished reading the article and placed the program into my special file.

I phoned Tamarah after the play to thank her for the ticket. She was amazed that the Ombra Mai Fu was in the play. She invited me to share with her a viewing of Wagner's Ring she had on the video tapes. She used to go every year to Seattle to watch the whole Ring of four major operas. Tamarah knew the music by heart and was familiar with libretto. Since her four years of age she was part of opera audiences in Stuttgart and strongly identified with Senta in The Flying Dutchman. Senta was another maiden that died.

155

The words of Martin Luther King Jr. are forever true: "If a man hasn't discovered something that he will die for, he isn't fit to live." Many of us who truly love, would offer our life first so our beloved could live. We are willing to do all kinds of sacrifices and go beyond our own limitations. In Love there are no limitations. In Love there is Life.

Ring

Wagner's Ring is about fifteen hours long. I couldn't place it into visiting hours with Tamarah, but I could borrow the tapes and watch them whenever possible for me. The operas were sang in German, but the subtitles were translated into English. I began to watch, read and listen to the treasure. I began to identify Tarot symbolism, and the mysteries of the nordic mythology. Every word, every line was perfectly chosen, matched by music. The costumes had messages with geometric designs, the names of characters had identified the persona.

Tamarah explained to me that the costume designs were chosen by King Ludwig II of Bavaria, who sponsored Wagner's work and most likely helped with the libretto. By every right the first performance of Lohengrin was private and the King himself occupied the swan boat in the opera Lohengrin. The famous "Swan King", whose favourite opera was Tristan and Isolde, the love story. But the King's most favourite was "The King of Lahore" by a French composer Jules Massenet.

Over several days I managed to view the whole Ring. The story of Sieglinde and Siegmund, who were twins and gave birth to Siegfried, touched me. Thanks to Valkyrie, the brave heart warrior, Siegfried survived his mother's death. He grew up in the wilderness, listening to the voices of nature that guided him to the Golden Stone, which was surrounded by fire and where Valkyrie was resting in a long deep sleep, wearing her armour. She was the Knight of the Golden Stone. She knew that the one who passes through the fire is her beloved. Siegfried fell in love with Brunhilde, and desiring his own transformation to become a king and worthy of her love, he put on a mask that transformed him into a king and took Brunhilde to his castle. The ring is returned to the Maidens of Rhein and everyone in the kingdom passes through the purifying fire.

Truly, the gold should never be in the hands of Nibelungs, the greedy and ignorant. The spiritual gold is for the kings and has to be available where nature intended it. The Creator's plan cannot be altered. Salvation cannot be stolen, neither faked. Regardless of what we believe that we are, or have, will perish with the first blow if it doesn't have its roots deep and high. Nothing built on sand can survive. We are powerless against the divine plan, the very blueprint of the Universe and of its activity. We cannot pretend to be gods. We can only become gods. That takes time and work. We have to prove ourselves worthy through our living, to earn the virtues, to become uncorruptable and the true warriors of Love and Light. Where are they, who are they?

On a vibrational level, like attracts like, we attract what we are, we attract what we think, we can create our own world within this one. We shall be wise, for we harvest what we sow. The mind has to be disciplined, it cannot indulge in fantasies and useless daydreaming, it must create progress. Thinking is a responsibility and once we learn to think well, according to the Divine Law, we participate in the creation of the New World. Not the one with one currency, plastic money, and a centralized government, but a world where all minds and hearts are in harmony. Essentiallly, we all want the same. We desire Love, Truth, Abundance. It is in the Plan since the beginning of the creation, it is ours to begin with. How do we go about it, then?

The wise minds of the past had left us legacy in their lives and work. I reached for a book in my bookcase and took out the Bress 103 sent to me by the Hermetic Library's curator two years earlier. On its cover there is an ancient drawing of the tree of life, with its roots set deeply in planetary bodies and the branches covered by leaves and fruit. The tree trunk is suspended by a hand coming from a cloud. The fruit on one side is harvested by male hands and the other side by female hands. Only the fruit picked by the female hands is ripe. The feminine side of creation is the catalyst to the harvest. Aaron told me that I have the power to recognize the fruit's ripeness. It is women's passive activity that will lead us to liberation. It is Opus Feminum.

Ingrid Heller

PART FOUR

OPUS FEMINUM

Ingrid Heller

A l c h e m y

.

Recently I've been hearing from several sources that the Patriarchal system has to change into the Matriarchal one, where the female, or the feminine energy, will be leading us into a future. We were held back by dominant male energy, and the creative, flowing, nurturing, fluidic and magnetic feminine energy may have to lead us beyond the present stagnant state. The Women's Liberation Movement was just a slight indication of the necessary change, regardless of how misleading it was to many wonderful women, wives, mothers. The change was never intended to become the battle of the sexes, neither a competitive race, but rather a cooperation through understanding and appreciation of feminine and masculine qualities to create a partnership into the future, on the way to completion.

There is a shortage of wise women who could do active work in this direction. In many cultures women are second class citizens, having no rights whatsoever. Those cultures reflect the attitude of masses in their consciousness. The leap forward was therefore upto the women of more developed nations with equal rights. It became the responsibility of women from the Northamerican continent, European women, and every "hell of a woman" from other cultures who dared to break the rule. Women are in possession of the holy grail and frequently they don't know it. Some began to complain about the males who desired them, who courted them making big promises, lied to them, did anything just to have them, even for one single night. All these men were seeking the feminine energy to enter their energy field, the one they couldn't bring forth themselves. They were seeking an experience that would take them beoynd the present one, they were seeking the way Home. Subconsciously, men know that women hold the key to the Iannua Coeli, the Gate to Heaven. Some women began to use this power in a selfish way. Blessed were the women who understood the purpose of this power and became the Brides of the Lamb. They studied, took workshops that guided them to understanding their role. I've met some. I also have met men who were fully aware about this process and who were consciously working on themselves toward Liberation. These men understood the power and the value of feminine energy and began to work with it in their relationships, in their daily living, and on their inner levels, transforming themselves toward the higher type - the spiritual and cosmic man. I've met some. They were alchemists on many levels, increasing their energy body and their awareness. The words processing, releasing, clearing, healing, and transforming became a part of their daily vocabulary.

Some alchemy was done at a mental level, some at a physical level and also at a sexual level. None of them could be compromised. Energy body was nurtured consciously, life force was never wasted, but used constructively. Martial arts, wholistic fitness, and yoga became a way of life for others. Thousands, millions of devotees live with awareness that they are responsible for their body's readiness to receive the higher energy. The Temple of God had to be built strong, The Church to house the Spirit had to be cleansed and ready. Our bodies had to be healthy and balanced to be able to receive higher frequencies and tune into a change without the resistance. The superconductive human being was the next step in evolution.

I was on my journey. I began to prepare. I wanted to be ready and didn't want to miss my, to me unknown, deadline. I added another therapy to my clinic: medical ozone. It is to assist people in healing, cleansing, building, and regenerating. I had the best generator and wonderful coaches. They were also very spiritual people, very much involved in higher knowledge of medicine, nature's laws and alchemy. I learned about the western alchemy and its applications. I knew for certain that by accelerating the evolution of the matter we accelerate the evolution of the spirit. The human being is responsible for this evolution. God is out of the picture now. He's done His job. We are gods now. We have to do our own healing. Healing means going back in time into a timeless dimension of the universal consciousness where there is true abundance on every level. We have to go back to our childhood, to the womb, and as a little children we find the way home. We have to go through that gate and experience the healing crisis first. The planet has to go through the same. It is inevitable. Prophecies in The Bible actually warn us about the healing crisis. Humanity has to experience the accumulation of its own deeds of collective unconscious. Some spiritually developed individuals had taken on themselves some of the planetary karma, the humanity's 'sins'. Jesus Christ was such an individual and there were many others in the history of mankind. They have capacity to transform and neutralize the karma of humanity. There are many of these individuals living among us today, at times in the darkest places of the largest cities, where they are needed the most. They qualified for this service, they had volunteered out of Love to do this work, because it has become their next step in evolution of their own consciousness. Everyone qualifies for their own mission. None of us is free unless all of us are free. With freedom there is responsibility.

There were no more secrets. All my tools were gathered and I was connecting to my soul family. The House of David of these times had opened its door lovingly and I knew that The Golden Age was coming. The Tree of Life from the middle of the Garden began to grow its fruit.

My children were still young. Joe and Jean were graduating from high school and choosing their careers. Jean was accepted in zoology study at the university, with the hope to continue in veterinary medicine. Joe was interested in mechanics. Monica went on to her favourite work and study of computer graphics. Maria and Andrew saw me a bit more, because I decided to work less hours and take better care of myself. I worked only six days a week and still loved every moment of it, but had to find the way to liberate myself to reach my goal. I knew that something would indicate the direction I was to take.

A friend brought me video tapes about The Flower of Life and Mercaba, another friend had a number of presentations by Stan Tennen from Meru Foundation for me. All of them had information I needed at that time. I felt like a dancer in the Dance of Creation, swayed by its rhythm and harmonies, enjoying the leading and the strength of my partner - my Soul. I was alive! I was grateful! I was in love!

Another friend, who had an interest in alchemy, brought me a book by Dione Fortune on The Mystical Cabbalah. I opened the book and see the word LAMEN. I read about the Holy Grail, Alpha and Omega, Rose Cross, and the Breast Plate. I read about balance, about our personal inner work, if we ever are to become triumphant. No one can do this work for us. This work we do alone, working on our virtues. Tamino in Magic Flute did his work and could not include Pamina in it, even though she was a catalyst. We must not forget that Tamino already defeated the dragon! Pamina had to do her own work and, later on, when they were united to pass the test of water and fire, they triumphed.

The thought of the pelican landing on the balancing beam and meeting me on the other side of it filled my mind. He was the alchemical bird. Alchemists use the term pelican for one of their glass tubes used during the process of making spagyrics.

I knew my direction The sooner I'd complete my work, the sooner I'd incarnate higher love and would meet my match. I found a meaningfull message daily in my Calendar of Spiritual Truth that I had on the clinic's reception counter. Tamarah gave it to me for Christmas. The words of wisdom were provided by a lady named Mary Hayes-Grieco. One of my favourite ones said: "Healing your body, your emotions, and your mind, so that the Spirit can shine through you, is the hardest work to undertake - but, what else do you have to do?"

"He who loves the world as his body, may be entrusted with the empire." - Lao-tzu

M e s s a g e s

One of the most rewarding human experiences is the awareness of being part of the whole. We are connected, none of us is alone. If one does something new, someone somewhere will do it also. If one is to cut the edges, there will be a supportive body of friends who will assist in some way to reach that goal. I witnessed it in many life situations, in solidarity, in healing, in bringing new progressive ideas and inventions. There is a constant activity, all vibrates at all times. I knew well that my next step will be shown to me. There was not as much exciting activity on the outer level, except that I'd been meeting new people, making new friends and getting better in my profession. There was a great deal of inner activity I was aware of. My dreams were informing me that all was well. Was I ever flying, being places, always networking.

Tamarah left for three months to Lahore and other cities in Pakistan. She bought a silk wardrobe of many beautiful colours to match her aura and to blend with the crowd. My friend Iris went to Israel to visit with her mother and to plan a possible future move to Tel-Aviv. I thought of moving to Chile, but when? I had a clinic to operate, deeply set roots in Alberta, many friends, and my children still needed me.

Monica phoned me after Christmas from Big White in Okanagan, where she was skiing with her boyfriend. She was getting engaged to get married. I was very happy for her and when I asked when, she said May 21st of '95. We were at the end of 1994. She promised that no more than one hundred guests would be invited. My parents got married on the same day fifty one years earlier.

Iris returned from Israel in the beginning of January. We spent more quality time together and I assisted her in the body detoxification she needed urgently. We always had a very special rapport together. We just flowed and laughed a lot. It was a very healing relationship for both of us. One evening, when I was done with my clients, I placed Iris in the steam cabinet while going through some exciting written material on the Hebrew alphabet provided by Meru Foundation. All of a sudden, Iris tells me to get her out of the cabinet, that she had to cool because some special energy was coming her way and she felt it was a message for me. I let her to step out and gave her free space. She sat down at my reception desk and began to write: all in Hebrew. I thought she wrote down her ideas. She finished one page and looked at me asking the question "When are you going to Chile?" I knew that something special was happening.

Never before did Iris do an automatic writing, neither channeling. She was aware about its dangers. She also knew how much I was against such practices.

"Iris," I asked, "what did you write?"

"Ingrid, this is my first time ever. It came in Hebrew! I couldn't write it in English!"

"Well, what is it? What did you write?"

Iris sat back, took a deep breath and explained. "Hebrew is structured differently than English, but I'll do my best. Sit here next to me and write.

Was I ever anxious. Before I was allowed to write the first word, she said it was about me and Ariel. She said I was to write a book about us and call it Ariel. When I asked if she was sure about the title, she said she wasn't, but I was definitely to use his real name in the book. Mystery embraced me again. I was beginning to write a very important message: "Know how to organize your affairs, put many roots down, and then tell the story right from the beginning as it happened. We are coming close to the "End of Times" and you must tell the story before then as many times as you can and write about it. Acknowledge where you are coming from, by receiving and accepting what is already here. Be open and remain open to another world and be aware about what is going on."

I was speechless for a while. I thanked the source that worked through Iris and I told her that I would call the book "The Divine Comedy II by Beatrice". She loved the title.

I had no more excuses. So many times I had an impulse to begin to write about my experience, frequently being encouraged by friends. I felt very strongly that one day I would have to find the time and do it, but in what form? Iris suggested a screen play, because that way I could reach the most of population. I had no idea how much work there was involved in writing a movie script. My heart wanted to write, but at that point I had no word processor, nor the time to write.

The following week my friend Gaetano came for a massage. He was all perky and excited. I thought he would relax during the massage, but his creative spirit kept on telling me that I had to write the story about Ariel and I, and get at it soon. "The world is waiting for it, Ingrid! It is a very important story! Do you realize how blessed you are to have this treasure of personal experience? All writers are just dreaming about something so true and deep. Look at them! They just write fictions! Ingrid, promise me that you will write it. You must write it!"

"Gaetano, you are my second messenger. Iris wrote a message in Hebrew for me. It said that I must write that story as it happened from the beginning."

"Exactly! Don't hold anything back. Tell it all!"

"Gae, I can only write some things, but the most important events will be there. I actually have a title: The Divine Comedy II by Beatrice."

Gaetano loved the title. He began to recite to me in Italian from Dante's Divine Comedy the exact part from the Canto XXV. He was a cultured Roman, immersed totally in Canadian life now. Gae was a writer himself, looking for inspiration, for his Beatrice.

In the same week one of my younger clients came for his massage. He changed his hairstyle and had a beard. When I entered the massage room, I complimented on his new look. He said that he would like to change his profession. He was an assistant movie director, and he was always very busy. I was surprised that he would be willing to give up the work that he loved so much. He explained that he would like to become a producer instead.

Alberta became a second Hollywood already. Some very important movies were filmed here and many Canadian writers and actors had a job. I asked my client whether it was difficult to become a producer. He replied that the hardest thing is to get a good movie script, that the money was always available. A good script was the key.

Was this a message to me to write a script instead of a novel? For a moment I was hesitant to say anything, but then I collected courage and told my client that I would have a very good script within two years. He felt it was a long time to wait.

"What would your script be about?"

"A true story. It is a bit mystical in nature. I would call it an esoteric thriller, or, a spiritual suspense."

He didn't respond, but brought me a sample of a movie script. I realized how much work there was ahead of me.

That same evening, when I got home, I saw a computer on our dining table. I asked Jean what it was all about. She said that her father gave it to her. I asked if she could teach me how to use the word processor, she vaguely agreed and warned me on the age of the computer.

"The age doesn't matter, Jean! As long as it is functional!"

She gave me a funny look. That girl had my mind.

One of my clients who was familiar with all computer systems taught me how to use the system in half an hour and that same evening I began to write. It took me quite a while to get used to a screen play version. I had to think for several people at the same time: actor, director, camera man, producer, lighting, budgeting, name it - it could give me a split personality. I realized what hard work it was, but I wanted to give it a try anyway.

Some friends did a proof reading and they loved the work. I was rushing to get ahead with it, so I could approach a professional screen writer for feedback.

Every evening I had something to look forward to. I spent hours in front of that old computer, until its sound and smell got to me. I took a three month break.

A wonderful opportunity came my way. Through the membership in Canadian Galleries I could have a trip to Amsterdam both ways, with hotel and breakfasts for nine days for only nine hundred and ninety dollars canadian, based on double occupancy. One lady friend, who'd never been to Europe and was fascinated by my reports on the Hermetic Library, wanted to come along. We traveled at the end of February, missing a terribly cold spell.

It was so wonderful to see all the people at the library, meet with Herman, Jacob's family, pay a visit to Nico and Key, and connect to friends in Paris. Jan lived outside Antwerp at this time. My friend was thrilled and found it difficult to absorb it all. Interestingly, she chose in the library writings that related to her spiritual growth of that time. We photocopied many pages of great manuscripts.

There was one interesting guest in the Library - a first timer. He looked for specific information on the Music of the Spheres He had a composer friend who desperately wanted to use the harmonies in his next composition. I told this young man about Genesis from the Hebrew Bible that could be musically transcribed. The Music of the Spheres was encoded right there. Both men were seeking power through the harmonies of creation itself. One has to hear it first, and then it can be written. The inner ear can hear it when the candidate is ready. Keys to creative power are within the keys of musical octaves.

At this time the library was in the hands of the Dutch government. I learned that the Ster company had financial problems. Their products were supplying airlines and with the reduction in air travel they earned less and had to borrow some money from the bank to carry on with the operation. The Library itself was the guarantee. Two years later it was for sale, but based on pressure from the public, the government agreed to finance the library. Ster had a new owner and Mr. Ritman still carried on with the library, collecting manuscripts of high value in knowledge. Herman, my friend, and I had incredible luck on our last day at the library. Mr. Ritman was just arriving when we were leaving. I introduced myself to him, thanked him for his service to humanity and asked what kind of help he would appreciate the most. He said "Books, I need books!"

One month after my return from Europe, Tamarah returned from Pakistan. On the way back to Canada she visited her mother in Stuttgart. Tamarah went to the local opera house three times a week. She relived the memories of her childhood, her fascination for Wagner's work, her admiration for costumes and colours. The whole trip brought a new beginning into her life. So much wisdom was spoken through her lips that many times I complimented on her growth. She was on her own Journey.

Iris was preparing for her move to Israel at the end of June, and I was preparing for my family's trip to Swift Current for Monica's wedding. All our needs had been met and that gave me the confirmation that I was on the right path. I was completing with my family's responsibilities, and with my House.

"By nature, men are nearly alike; by practice, they get to be wide apart." – Confucius

The Tree of Life at Eden Clinic, aerographic painting by Alberto Blázquez is at left.

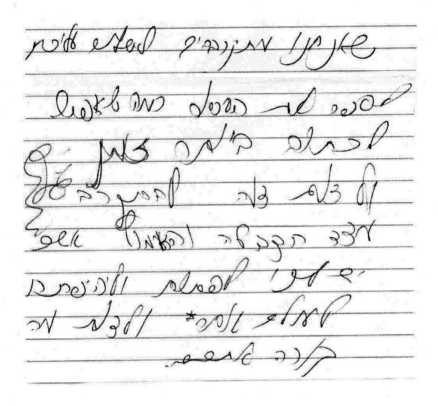

The message from Iris in Hebrew (the first part).

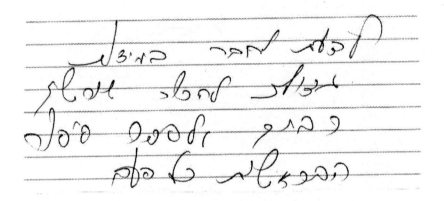

The message from Iris in Hebrew (the second part).

P e n t a g r a m

Monica was the most beautiful bride I'd seen for a long time. She carried herself gracefully and was a gift to her very handsome husband. Maria was the flower girl, Andrew was the ring boy. Jean was the bride's maid and Joe lit up the candles during the ceremony.

Monica became another Canadian home base for my children. I had only three children left to take care off. Joe was pretty independent. Jean was so far surviving on summer earnings and scholarships. She was an honour student.

Upon my arrival at the clinic, right after the long weekend, I noticed that my clepia plant was blooming for the first time. She had a cluster of eighteen four inch long stems ending with a five pointed star of a pink colour. The flowers looked like they were made of wax. They are very special plants, doing well near eastern or southern windows. Monica phoned me from the airport. The newlyweds were going for their honeymoon to Hawaii. She and her husband visited us on the way back and they both witnessed the beautiful blossom, which dried completely three days later.

In the beginning of June I traveled with Iris to Edmonton. She went to her native city to say good-bye to her aunt and cousin, the only Canadian relatives she had. I went to take a two day "Screen Play Writing Seminar" and to get in touch with my friend Wayne and his fiancée Heather.

We left very early in the morning and arrived on time. The lecture room was filling up. Most of the seminar was presented by Herbert Wright, who was involved in writing Star Trek - Tne Next Generation. He introduced us to the truth of the screen writing business. Stories that deal with humanitarian issues, high ideals, the nice tales, do not sell. We are writing majorly for an American audience, which gets stimulated by at least one bloody scene, possible rape, child molestation, basically anything violent enough to keep the 'couch potato viewer' interested to stay on the same channel during the first commercial. The remote control has the power. There were some other people, besides myself, who chose to stick to their principles and not to succumb to ugliness and money games. Herbert knew the reality of the business. Some information was encouraging. Science fiction, stories about aliens and cowboys, were selling.. We were introduced to a couple of Canadian agents.

During our lunch I showed Herbert my "mini arc of the covenant", which we call a beamer. He was fascinated by it and wanted one after I explained to him how it worked. Basically, it is a magnifier of creative energy, a tool to assist us before we become magnifiers ourselves.

Herbert loved the explanation on the octaves of elements, and how the beamer is layered inside and filled with noble gases. The staff of the High Priest in its tiny version, the inexhaustible battery. First to ninth octave had its representation in the elements that were exciting each other endlessly, magnetizing each other by their own nature throughout the circle of creation, working with the thought and purpose of its user: purifying, restructuring. The tool for the healer and the alchemist. Naturally, Herbert wanted one. I gave him mine. He was somehow surprised. He had to promise me to use it for good. "Once you become a creator", I told him, "your creation will return to you. It has your own and personal essence. Therefore, it is only yours to deal with. Now, do you understand why only good can be created?" He understood and wanted some written material on it. I promised to bring it the next day.

It was easy to live upto this promise. Wayne actually makes beamers himself and many other wonderful "cosmic toys". I got another beamer for myself and a bunch of written information for Herbert.

It was lovely to stay overnight at Wayne's house. He had ornaments there, that Atlanteans may have used in their households, with the sacred geometry, crystals, gold, with many Stars of David and some Pentagrams. Both emanate a powerful energy, but the pentagram is known to repel negative energy. Mr. Ritman's company Ster had the same kind of pentagram in its seal, like the shape of clepia blossoms.

Herbert reminded me of my promise in the morning. I passed him the folder with very interesting text and he was happy to have some material for science fiction. The seminar was worthwhile. I met creative positive people and a couple of screen-play writers from Calgary. One of them lived just around the corner from my clinic and he promised that he'd take a look at my script.

On the way home Iris and I sang together. She enjoyed the Bach music I sang to her, and the folklore songs from my country and Russia. Iris was an Ashkenazic Jewess whose roots were in Russia for hundreds of years. The music of that country was enchanting her, healing her, it was known to her cellular memory. Harmonies and instruments our ancestors used to listen to can assist in healing our family tree of all living relatives and descendants. All the healing we do personally we do for our family tree. There is always one in each family who is a bit ahead, "the weirdo" that is a bit "off the wall".

Business slowed down at the clinic. I didn't quite know how to read it, or explain it. It was unusual. I had time to write, to connect to some people after a long pause, and to contemplate. Suddenly, I began to miss Chile so much, that tears filled my eyes and my body was in anguish of nostalgia. What is this all about?

Two days later one of my clients called me with very important information, which triggered the change. I was sitting at my desk and before me opened a scene of my immediate future. I was to sell the clinic and move to Chile. When? October '96.

I had something to plan for again. There was no way I could be bored with my life, or anyone who was sharing my journey. It was always exciting. I phoned Eduardo and told him about my plan. He was quite excited and didn't object to the idea. He would be going home. We had a joint custody and none of us could take the children out of the province or into another country without the other's consent. I announced my plans to a few friends and when they asked about the sale of the clinic, I told them that it would be indicated to me somehow when to start to advertise.

Iris left at the end of June for Israel. She was nervous about it. She burned all bridges, just like I did years ago, when I moved to Chile. She knew from me how powerful these moves are and how to use this opportunity for personal and spiritual growth. Iris hoped to find her beloved among her people.

I didn't receive any communication from Ariel yet, neither on our seventh anniversary. Now I had the understanding of 'lamen' and the situation. Instead of hearing from Ariel, I received three marriage proposals from three friends, to which I said "No" because I was leaving the country. Before contemplating any marriage, or a serious relationship, I had to complete what I was already involved in. I needed to go to Chile with another hundred percent commitment. I had to go back to the point of seeing Ariel last, or first, to connect again with the energy that would magnify on the location of the experience itself. In Ariel's poem Vocabulary he writes: "When two of them met far away on unfamiliar street corner, they could not know if it was a first meeting, or a farewell..." I was going to go to that street corner of Ahumada and Huérfanos, feel the stones under my soles, rewind the tape, but never rewrite the script.

At the end of July my friend was getting married to a very nice gentleman. She was on her path full of good intentions and truly deserved the security that came with this relationship. I went to witness the ceremony in the morning and in the afternoon I went to the clinic to assist my clients. The clepia plant was in full bloom again! The same blossom, which was completely dried, resurrected into twenty-one star stems. Is this plant's consciousness trying to tell me something? Does it bloom on wedding days?

I checked with a horticulturist to learn about the pattern of this plant. It blooms when it is mature and the water and light conditions are right. It is the only plant he knew that resurrects its blossoms from the dead ones and keeps on adding the number of stems. This time the blossoms began to dry on the fourth day. The fragrant pentagrams blooming in its season had been going through the cycles of death and rebirth, in the wheel of life.

"What do you need to heal in order to trust the present moment?" - Mary Hayes-Grieco

Prelude

Since it was my last year in Calgary, I had to catch up with some missing experiences. For three years I stayed away from singing, due to long working hours, and I wanted to update my dancing techniques. I was back with the choir, which was going to do my favourite Bach's B-minor Mass, and with the Debut Opera group, that worked on the popular opera choruses this time. Participating in both of them was pleasurable. We had an excellent instructor in the dance classes and I learned to dance better.

I tried to see my older children more. Joe lived with his pretty girlfriend and Jean shared an apartment with her boyfriend, who was also a student. Monica was studying in Edmonton. Most of her trips on weekends were to Swift Current to meet with her husband. Hanna and I phoned each other less. We were slowly drifting apart. I didn't expect everyone of my friends to tune in. I lived too quickly, in reality I was experiencing several lifetimes in one incarnation.

Winter was very cold and long. Just another good reason to leave. I love sun and heat. I had always loved to grow flowers and vegetables, to hear the birds singing, and to be outdoors. We were an indoor society and it showed in public health. We had a problem.

The clepia bloomed in September again, but not once since then. The first week of March she bloomed in several clusters. That day I opened the Yellow Pages and looked up the business broker. The first intuitive choice is the best choice. He was interested and he came. A hard working and intelligent man, who understood the value of my services. Mine was his first wholistic clinic he was to sell. Naturally, there were very few of us and none with my combination of services.

We had interested buyers from the first day of advertisement. They all had medical background. In May he brought a lady who was a buyer. She wanted it badly and she got it. It was time to let 'my baby' go. It was sold to the first of September.

A very dear friend was returning from Macedonia back to Yellowknife and transferred in Calgary. She, her husband, baby daughter, and I met at the airport. They brought me a gift - a red Macedonian wine that was called "I Miss the South". It was named after a poem written by an exiled Macedonian poet while in Moscow. The label with the poem was attached to the bottle. I missed the south.

During the last months at the clinic I had to complete with some unfinished affairs and work further on my book. I was writing a novel afterall. Screen writer friends suggested that it was far too good to put in a movie, perhaps it could create a series, but the philosophical value would be lost. Besides, it would be a very expensive movie to produce. I felt much more comfortable about writing a novel. My mistakes can be corrected by an editor and I can add a documentation and pictures to prove the true story. It was my first novel, and knowing from the experience that the first time is always exciting, I was all for it. It was like a prelude for my first symphony.

.

"In this world we cannot have security. We can have serenity." - Mary Hayes-Grieco

Santiago

There couldn't have been a better timing. Canada and Chile were preparing for the Free Trade Agreement and for the first time ever the Canada EXPO was to be held in Santiago in the beginning of December. I registered on behalf of alternative medicine and was preparing for the right representation. I needed to prepare some promotional material in Spanish and English, and possibly in French. I had another reason to go to Chile! Through a friend I had rented a furnished apartment in the heart of Santiago by the Catholic University and the General Hospital, so, I had the address, and phone number and could have started to present my activity correctly. I certainly intended to continue with my work in Chile, network and introduce seminars of alternative therapies, and organize my life so there would be balance. I needed time for my children, recreation, and social life.

The whole month of September was dedicated to clearing my household, organizing a temporary storage for my books, photo albums, correspondence, which was reducing its volume with each move, and many sentimental items accumulated over the years. Among the stored items were two wine bottles. One was a Macedonian "I Miss the South", and the other a Bulgarian Sophia year 1988. These wines were to be opened on a very special celebration. Everything else was being given away to my children or friends. Bridges were being burnt. There was no return into any security. Our plane tickets had a return flight for the next Christmas, to visit with my other children. I was leaving behind about ten boxes and stored them in Tamarah's house. Suitcases were packed for the most part for several months now.

It was exciting. I had some time for social life yet, to get to know my friends better and to have a clear idea about which relationship would likely survive the change. I pretty well knew what to expect of everyone. By changing my energy, I was surfacing emotional responses in others. It naturally occurs. It happened in the year '90, when after twenty-one years I visited my country and stayed at my mother's place. I stayed with her for three days only. My energy was unknown to her and she experienced some difficulty. Many issues she refused to deal with in the past were coming to her conscious mind and she was confused and very reactive. I became her mirror and she was not ready to see the truth. I had to leave and stay with other relatives and friends who were more progressive people. Many people in my country are emotionally injured and without faith they closed in, finding it difficult to relate. I was thinking about the Chilean people of today. How are they dealing with the economical changes, democratic system, and a new opening to the world? Are they still happy? Do they understand what is happening with their country's future economically, socially, and ecologically? Do they have enough spirit left in themselves to be awake and feel the truth? Could they connect to the experiential genetic memory and be aware? That reality I would have to discover on my own once I was there. I would listen to the media, I would listen to the silence, and in the serenity of my own interior I would know the truth. As Buddha said: "Three things cannot be hidden: the sun, the moon, and the truth."

In October I took the children to the west coast and Victoria. We stayed in motels and with friends in Langley. Victoria kept us well entertained for two days. We left just before the typhoon hit the island and the coast.

The drive through the Rockies is breathtaking. So much beauty is revealed, that in few hours one cannot keep up. A human being has the capacity to take in little by little, step by step. That way the emotional response has the potential to escalate toward the ecstasy, otherwise, the experience may be too overwhelming and perceived as unreal, or as a dream. Looking at those gorgeous mountains, that I never climbed because there was no man to share it with, no one who could talk to me with his eyes and feelings in tranquility in the midst of sacredness of nature itself, I asked myself a question: Will I ever be able to share them with Ariel? Or, will there be another 'Ariel', the one who is to be my partner in life? Do I really understand the mystery of the 'twin souls'? Do we grow next to the one who is like us and has the same blueprint? Climbing the third mountain is an exciting adventure, but, what if there is a cliff instead of a peak, and the view of another valley and another plain opens before us? Are we expected to jump into death trusting that our wings will carry us toward the next mountain across the valley? Could I trust in the same way I trust in my flying dreams, having full control over my acrobatic movements, landings, take offs? Winston Churchill once said: "It is a mistake to look too far ahead. Only one link in the chain of destiny can be handled at a time." I decided to follow his advice. Living in the present was always the secret to the mastery of life; why should I worry about what the next step will be? NOW is the most important moment in our Journey. There is its beginning and its end.

I had a few days yet before our flight, with many wonderful moments to enjoy. The clearing of my unresolved past would happen on its own in the moments of beingness itself. I was open to living. I was to leave these mountains behind, the snowy hills I skied on with so much enjoyment and feeling of freedom, one of the most magical places on the planet. There was before me another magic, a new stage, a new world and continent.

The last few days before the flight were more intense than I expected. I had to accept, understand and forgive in a hurry. I couldn't carry any baggage with me onto my next stage of life. There were some tears, some sadness, but I had to let go and make the unpleasant experiences history. Only through the human mind can we neutralize what transpired. Forgiveness is the key. I had a long trip before me and had to be calm to give my children support. They were leaving their friends behind as well, trusting their Mother and Father.

On the flight from Los Angeles to Santiago I had more time to relax and think. Maria was sitting next to me by the window. Andrew was sitting next to Eduardo right behind us. The Chilean airline service was excellent. I was tasting the Chilean wine, swiveling its flavour around the walls of my sensuous palate and tongue. I was tasting, again, the land of my beloved, the land that was a catalyst for my comedy. The land of fishermen, huasos, artisans, musicians, writers, and poets. The land that trembles with earthquakes, where volcanos erupt, where the rays of sun crack the fields and the rains wash down the hills. I was to embrace that land and make it my own. It was Maria's birthplace and Andrew's cradle in my womb. In this land I'd connect to him who was my inspiration - my Dante. The comedy is almost over. The curtain shall be drawn. The director closes the script and I, the Beatrice, the three times blessed, am between the Earth and Heaven, being carried by the wings, still swiveling the wine, speechless. No words are being spoken. There is only an appreciation of the essence and experience itself, the ability to breathe and to hear the blood rushing through the arteries. The world within, the unspoken, the infinite and absolute. I am that I AM. So are you!

To be continued in another time and space ...

"Beatrice" pastel by Odilon Redon, 1885

About the Author

Ingrid Heller was born in 1946 in Czechoslovakia. She was interested in the music and arts since her early childhood, and in writing poetry and essays later in her teens, but abandoned her passion and beloved country when the Warsaw pact armies invaded Czechoslovakia in 1968. She has resided in Calgary, Alberta, Canada since 1969, where she raised her five children. She also lived in Chile for three years with her family. Brought up and educated in an atheist society, Ingrid looked to nature and the human being for answers to the mysteries of life. Fascinated by both the complexity and simplicity of nature's laws and human existence, and their physical and spiritual expression, she eventually became a naturopathic and wholistic practitioners. She practices in Calgary.

Ingrid is presently working on "Footprints in the Andes" and looks forward to writing a collection of erotic 'memoirs of golden girls' in "The Wise Pussy Tales".

"The Common Sense Health Manual" is derived from her professional work and is to be published by the end of 2002.

Printed in the United States
1018400002B/1-78